PENGUIN BOOKS
THE FIG TREE

Aubrey Menen was born in 1912 in London, of Indian and Irish parentage, and was educated at University College, London, where H.G. Wells encouraged him as a writer. He worked at several jobs—at various times he was drama critic, stage director, radio broadcaster, press officer, scriptwriter, education officer for the Government of India and head of the Motion Picture Department for the J. Walter Thompson Company, London—before turning to writing full time. He published several novels including *The Prevalence of Witches* (1947), *The Stumbling Stone* (1949), *The Backward Bride* (1950), *The Duke of Gallodoro* (1952), *The Abode of Love* (1956), *SheLa* (1962) and *A Conspiracy of Women* (1966). He also wrote a number of non-fiction books and an autobiography *The Space Within the Heart* (1970). His book *Four Days of Naples* (1979) is to be filmed in Hollywood and his satirical *Rama Retold* (1954) is being prepared for Broadway. Aubrey Menen died in Trivandrum in 1989.

AUBREY MENEN
The Fig Tree

PENGUIN BOOKS

Penguin Books (India) Ltd, 72-B Himalaya House,
23 Kasturba Gandhi Marg, New Delhi-110 001, India
Penguin Books Ltd, Harmondsworth, Middlesex, England
Viking, Penguin Inc, 40 West 23rd Street, New York, N.Y. 10010, U.S.A.
Penguin Books Australia Ltd, Ringwood, Victoria, Australia
Penguin Books Canada Ltd, 2801 John Street, Markham, Ontario, Canada L3R 1B4
Penguin Books (N.Z.) Ltd, 182-190 Wairau Road, Auckland 10, New Zealand

First published by Chatto & Windus 1957
Published in Penguin Books 1963
Reissued in Penguin Books India 1989
Reprinted 1989
Copyright © The Estate of Aubrey Menen 1988, 1989
All rights reserved
Made and printed in India by Ananda Offset Pvt Ltd.

For Philip Dallas

AT the time when these events took place, there was an extraordinary fig tree, which grew on a terrace that overlooked the blue waters of the Bay of Salerno, in Italy. Fig trees had been growing in this spot for two thousand years, but nobody had seen a tree such as this one.

It was not big: but it was lush. Its leaves were as thick as those of a rubber-plant; its trunk shone like the coat of a well-groomed horse. Its figs were coloured a royal purple and they were as big as grapefruit.

This is the story of that fig tree, and of the man who made it, whose name was Harry Wesley.

*

Harry was the serious son of serious parents who went to chapel and led sober, industrious, and very respectable lives in a suburb of London. When he was still a boy he conceived a great admiration for scientists, whom he considered the most important people in the world, as we all do. When any of his heroes spoke on the radio or wrote in the newspapers (as they frequently did) he studied what they had to say most attentively. This made him a more serious boy than ever, because he learned that the human race was in a very bad way. It would either wantonly destroy itself through war (they said) or else just as wantonly produce too many babies and so starve itself to death because there would not be enough for everybody to eat.

Young Harry did not feel he could do much about stopping people destroying themselves in war, but their other possible fate deeply engaged his thoughts. By the time he was fourteen he had decided that when he grew up he would save humanity. Thus when other boys of his age dreamed of being Olympic champions or unbeatable boxers, Harry dreamed of grateful nations unveiling statues of himself as their saviour. To be a saviour he had, of course, to be a scientist, and this he made up his mind to be.

From that time onwards, he allowed nothing to get in the way of his ambition. He gave up going to chapel, because he noted that scientists had little use for religion; he gave up the Boy Scouts, because they were too cheerful for his serious frame of mind; and he gave up football, which he enjoyed, because it took up too much of his time.

On his sixteenth birthday his headmaster called him to his study and asked him in a paternal way if he had given any thought as to what he wanted to do in life. Harry said, in his serious treble:

'Yes, sir, I have. I wish to invent an oral contraceptive.'

His headmaster at first thought that Harry had an exceptionally dirty mind. But on making inquiries among the staff, he was told that, on the contrary, for a schoolboy he had an exceptionally clean one. He therefore reluctantly granted Harry's request to take extra chemistry lessons, but, as a precaution, he insisted that Harry resumed his football.

*

Harry threw himself into his studies. Unencumbered by religion, or camping under canvas, and playing football for no more than the necessary one game a week, he made great progress. He carried off a brilliant series of scholarships and in due course won the right and the money to go to a college in London University that specialized in science. Here he was interviewed by an elderly Dean whose task was to find out, unobtrusively, in what direction his work in the college should go. The Dean had a winning manner and he soon got Harry to talk about himself and his ambitions. Charmed by his questioner and sipping the first glass of sherry he had tasted in his life, Harry confessed that the dream of his life was to be present while a grateful nation – or several – unveiled a statue to him for having invented an oral contraceptive. His questioner considered this for a moment and then said :

'My dear Mr Wesley, I am given to understand that already there is available a wide range of contraceptives. They must all have been invented by somebody – clever fellows, too, when you come to think of it. But I don't recall any of them ever getting a statue. Suppose you think the matter over, Mr Wesley, and we'll have another chat tomorrow.'

Harry went away and told himself that this was the first man who had ever treated his ambition seriously, and, next, what the man had said was right. But he was not deflected from his purpose of saving humanity. If it was inadvisable, from the point of view of deathless fame, to secure that the human race had less babies, he could still see to it that it had more food. That, surely, was an eminently respectable thing to do. He had already studied what was being done in the matter, and he decided that the solution would lie in altering the chemistry of plant cells.

He went back to the elderly man with the winning manner. His interviewer agreed that this was a much more respectable choice, and sent him off to see the greatest living authority on the subject. This distinguished man told him that some ten thousand other people were at that moment working away with exactly the same idea. He thought that something was bound to be discovered soon. He recommended Harry to take his degree and then to try his hand. He said that the thing to do was to keep a sharp eye open on his fellow-researchers' work and if he was lucky he might be able to nip in at the right time and take the credit. He assured him that this was how the thing was done. He said that he, himself, had two or three times almost made an important discovery, but somebody had always been nippier than he.

Harry took the distinguished authority's advice to heart. He got his degree and then a doctorate. That done, he went on to fulfil his life's ambition. He studied hard, he worked hard, and he kept a sharp eye open. At the age of thirty-two he was awarded a Nobel Prize. His colleagues were profoundly indignant, but the distinguished authority assured him that in the world of science, they always were. He told him he would probably never make another contribution to knowledge in his life, because science was a young man's game. The best thing to do, he said, and the most tactful, was to take a job abroad. That was how Harry Wesley came to the Gulf of Salerno, in Italy, and made his extraordinary fig tree.

*

The most profitable export of Italy is fruit. Harry's Nobel Prize had been given to him because he had found a fluid which, injected into fruit trees, would greatly increase their yield. It happened that an election was pending and the current Government was being attacked for having done nothing for the peasants. The leader of the ruling party therefore had the idea of asking Harry to come to Italy and manufacture his fluid there. The invitation was spectacular, and the election, for this and other reasons, was won.

The Government, once more in power, had no real intention of carrying out the scheme, which they feared would be expensive and which they knew would cost them an effort. But, by a rare chance, one of the Under-Secretaries was an energetic man. He was called Andrea Pozzo, and he set up a pilot laboratory for making Harry's fluid, largely by stealth and wholly on credit.

When Harry came to Rome, he was not received with any great show of official enthusiasm, except by Pozzo, who did his best to make him welcome. But Harry, piqued at his reception, did not like Pozzo at all. He found him very foreign in his ways. He was not surprised to learn from him that he owed his position in the Government to the fact that he was the nephew of one Cardinal Capuano – in itself a very foreign thing to be.

But he approved of the laboratory – though he did not approve of it being blessed by the Cardinal – and he got down to work. He found that his colleagues and assistants were well-trained and helpful. Some of them were young women. One of Pozzo's most foreign acts was to tell Harry, confidentially, that he had personally seen that some at least of the women were pretty. Harry was embarrassed. He had been prepared since his adolescence for waves of sexual desire to throw him off his work from time to time, as it did others. But he had experienced no waves: the most that he had ever felt was a gentle lapping at the shore.

There were indeed some laboratory assistants who were beautiful in the ripe, Italian style. But Harry did not trouble them, and they took little notice, in that sense, of Harry. He was, in any case, scarcely a handsome man. His face was amiable, but vaguely composed. He had sandy hair, a good, but not fine, forehead, pale grey eyes, and an indeterminate nose. His was the sort of face that one feels might do better with a moustache and, then again, one feels it might not.

Undisturbed therefore by any romantic interludes, Harry produced sufficient of his fluid to make a test. It was the season when figs were just appearing on the trees in the warmer part of the country, so Harry packed his bags and went south to make an extended trial in a place that Pozzo had found for him. In a short time he had produced a tree which was a wonder to see.

PART TWO

THE terrace on which the wonderful fig tree grew was the one ugly thing in a scene of surpassing beauty. Limestone cliffs, sculptured into hollows and pinnacles of an endless variety, towered away to the north. To the south, other terraces set with vines and olives made steps down to the Mediterranean Sea. White farmhouses shone here and there against the dark-foliaged trees that were sometimes peppered with blossoms and sometimes bent under the weight of lemons and oranges. It was very quiet, save for the rustle of the sea against the rocks below.

On Harry's terrace, however, there were no vines. They had been rooted up. There were no olive trees, or rather there was nothing left of them but their stumps. Instead, the terrace grew a strange crop of measuring devices that marked the wind, the sun, and such rain as fell. There were cameras that whirred momentarily every few minutes, took pictures, and shut themselves off. Rods sunk in the ground sent electric messages to automatic pens. Sprinklers guarded against an unusual drought, lamps that burned blue took the place of the sun if it stayed exceptionally long behind a cloud. The tree itself, with thin metal slivers sunk here and there in its silky bole, stood alone, save for one other growing thing. This was another fig tree, a flourishing one, but looking wan and sickly beside the other because, although it shared all the coddling, it had not been given Wesley's acid.

To Harry Wesley, this unlovely clutter was the most beautiful plot of land he had ever seen. He was happy and contented at last. He lived in a small farmhouse that had been summarily adapted for him by running in some simple sanitation and a shower. He spent most of his days checking his instruments, taking minute samples from his tree, and injecting the acid, a delicate and still uncertain procedure which varied, according to complex equations, with the readings on his instruments. Part of his contentment came from the fact that slowly shaping in his mind each day was a simpler system which any farmer could use. He left his farmhouse and terrace only once a week when he went to Salerno to study his slides and samples on an electronic microscope that filled a whole room, and enabled him to glimpse, if not steadily observe, the very molecules of which the living matter of his fig tree was made. He came back pleased, for things went just as he had hoped.

He was so absorbed in his work that he barely noticed that none of the neighbouring farmers spoke to him. The men who had come from Rome and Milan to set up the apparatus had told them what Wesley was doing. But naturally they did not believe what slick men in city suits told them. The farmers bided their time and watched. The first things that struck them as bogus were the film cameras. These were photographing a tree. Everybody knew that genuine film cameras were meant to photograph actresses. Their suspicions were confirmed when they observed that the so-called cameras worked both day and night. For the night-time photography, lights would suddenly blaze on and as suddenly be extinguished, a process which went on throughout the hours of darkness. The whole face of the cliff behind the terrace was thus fitfully illuminated every few minutes or so. Under this cliff ran the path by which the farmers, on very dark nights, took their barrels of wine to secret rendezvous for sale and thus avoided paying the tax. Harry's job was clear. He was an exciseman. It was clever, they thought, using a foreigner. But he spoke Italian well. He might not be as English as he looked. They forbade their families to speak to him and as for themselves did no more than wish him good morning and good night, with knowing smiles.

When a foundling girl of the village who cleaned Harry's house and cooked his spaghetti mentioned that, for an exciseman, he was growing some very good figs she was sharply told to mind her own business. That tree, she was informed with a great deal of swearing, had grown enormous figs for years: as far back, she was told, as the time when her unknown mother was begetting her in a ditch with a drunken sailor. After that the figs grew and grew, but she held her peace.

*

Harry had one neighbour who was not a farmer. He lived directly below him, on the terraces that bordered the sea. He lived in a large house that had been much added to, with porticos, balconies, and loggias, and the terraces that lay round it had been turned into an extravagantly fine Italian garden. Harry asked about its owner, and the foundling girl, reluctant to say anything at all, finally told him that he was an American, who had money. The most notable thing about him, according to the girl, was that he did nothing at all from one day's end to another.

'Everybody,' she said, 'calls me the laziest slut on the coast, and so I am, may the good God forgive me. I like doing nothing from time to time, and if the weather's fine. But if I did nothing like that American down there, morning, noon, and night, rain or shine, I should go stark, staring, raving mad.'

This was unfair. It was true that Harry's neighbour was an American: it was true that he had money. But he did not do nothing. He ate two square meals a day: or rather, they were square only in that they were substantial. In design they were the most curvilinear and the most elaborate baroque.

Harry's neighbour was called Joe Bellman. Joe was very fond of food. It cannot be said that Joe had made an art of cooking. Painters paint, sculptors use a chisel, and even the most advanced composers sometimes play the piano.

Joe never touched a pot or a pan, or indeed ever entered his heavily staffed kitchen. This was because next to food the thing he liked best was having no occupation at all.

The Bellmans were a large family and were extensively occupied. They made things all day long, and lay in bed thinking of their factories making things all night. They made chemicals and plastics; tractors and limousines; paper and cement, according to which branch of the family they were in. Only Joe made nothing at all. Only Joe could never understand how things work. Only Joe slept tranquilly at night, having made nothing all day long, not even his own bed. He was such a useless member of the family that Uncle Paul (the richest Bellman and known as Oom Paul to them all) said that Joe was probably a writer. Joe dutifully agreed that he probably was, and tried to make a book. But when Oom Paul asked him how the book was coming along, he had replied, 'Very well, Oom Paul, but it's just that I don't seem to see how writers do these bits where someone says something and then someone answers back. I've tried, but it doesn't seem to work.'

Oom Paul banished him to Europe on the spot to look after the family interests there, which were practically nothing.

One day Joe had been driving Oom Paul along the very stretch of coast where Harry was growing his fig tree. A laughing boy had thrown a wild flower into their car and it had fallen on Oom Paul's lap.

'Why did he do that?' asked Oom Paul.

'Because he's happy and he likes you,' said Joe.

'Oh,' said Oom Paul. He examined the flower attentively. 'What sort of flower is it?'

'It's a thistle,' said Joe.

'Oh!' said Oom Paul. 'It's not a very good thistle.'

This answer had made Joe so sad that he determined at that very moment that he would leave his family for ever and settle down on that very spot.

This he did and he lived happily ever after until Harry grew his fig tree, for Harry's fig tree caused him the most strenuous and difficult hours of his life.

*

He was profoundly alarmed when Harry started up his apparatus on top, so to speak, of his head. He would gaze up at Harry, and Harry would look down at him. Harry saw a short plump man, very red all over, with the figure of a well-fed twelve-year-old boy, who spent most of his day lying in the sun or splashing about in the sea. When they met in the road or in the village piazza, Joe would nod to Harry and trot past him on his short legs. Harry, writing home to one of his colleagues, said his neighbour was standoffish, but did not seem a bad fellow. He tried to describe him but failed, since he had no talent for that sort of thing. The Countess della Quercia, who had, said that Joe looked like the historian Edward Gibbon, parboiled.

Countess della Quercia, who was one of Joe's few friends on the coast, was able to set his fears at rest. He had asked his servants what was going on, but they had long ago come to a compact among themselves never to tell their master the truth, because it put him off his food. They concocted the story that it was to do with a film, thinking that their master, like themselves, would be delighted with the idea of beautiful film stars swimming in the bay. Joe, who had not been inside a cinema for twenty years, refused to eat dinner. Countess della Quercia, arriving next morning to do Joe's accounts and pay his bills (for this was something he could never bring himself to do), found the staff with faces suitable for a house of mourning.

But she had met Harry, and liked him, and she told Joe what he was doing. Joe, full of remorse at having cut so distinguished a man, asked him to dinner and asked the Countess as well.

It was most successful. Harry had never dined with a countess. He had, in theory, egalitarian views, but these were quickly assuaged because the Countess, as she always did, began the conversation by saying that her family went back to the thirteenth century and that she, personally, was dead flat broke. Continental aristocracy might have put Harry into a democratic huff. Decayed aristocracy was just, as Harry said to himself, the ticket.

As for his host, he all but fell in love with him. There was more of the eighteenth century about him than his resemblance to Edward Gibbon. Like most Americans, his manners were formal, but unlike the majority of his countrymen's civilities, his were secure. His accent, too, of which he was proud, was a relic from that period, which has survived (to the shame of the present-day English with their mechanical bleat) in a few of the older universities. Above all, Joe barely seemed to know that the modern world existed: not, at least, its darker aspects. He had the comfortable optimism that died when men began to wear trousers instead of breeches. Joe often fancied he would have looked well in breeches. He had the leg for it; a short one, he admitted, but still, the leg for it.

He liked Harry and soon got into the habit of asking him each evening, usually to a *tête-à-tête*, for there were not many residents of the coast whose company Joe liked enough to have them at his table. They would eat Joe's elaborate dinner, and then sit on one of Joe's many balconies, looking out at the sea and the moon. Behind them, hidden by trees, Harry's cameras would intermittently whirr, and his lights shine for brief moments. Behind these, higher up the mountains, the farmers would carry their illicit wine to the trysting-place, in short runs, for they had mastered the timing of the lights and were hugely pleased at the way they were outwitting the excise spy.

On one of these occasions, Joe relaxed for a while his

studied lack of interest in the world about him and talked
hesitantly of Harry's job.

'It's a strange thing,' said Joe. 'Here we are sitting on a
loggia together. The night is perfect. There is a full moon.
The dinner was excellent. At least,' he said, correcting himself, 'I hope you found it good.'

'Very good indeed,' said Harry.

'Thank you. As I was saying, here we are sitting quite
happily in each other's company. At least,' he said, correcting himself again, 'I am happy in *your* company.'

Harry, unable to cope with these delicacies, but enjoying
them, mumbled some agreeable noises round his cigar.

'And yet,' said Joe, 'you're a scientist. A most distinguished scientist, of course.'

'Dunno so much,' said Harry. 'A lot of chaps get the
Nobel Prize, you know. I looked them up. One chap got it
for having found the cause of cancer. He was a pure charlatan, although perhaps he didn't know it. He said the cause
was worms.'

Joe winced and was glad that his manservant came round
at that moment with the brandy tray. As he poured himself
another glass he reflected that nobody nowadays, not even
a thoroughly nice chap like Harry, knew what to talk about
– and what not to talk about – after dinner.

'That is most interesting,' he said, 'and some other time I
would like to hear more about it. But what I was going to
say was that you are the first scientist I have ever got on
with. My family employs droves of them and they think very
highly of them. I'm afraid I don't. They're always upsetting
things, changing things about. Of course you're English, and
that makes a great deal of difference. I like the English. A
very civil people in my opinion. There is only one thing
wrong with them, and that is they don't understand the importance of food. But d'you see, you *do*. As far as I can
gather you have spent your life inventing *better* food.'

'Well,' said Harry, 'I suppose so. In an abstract way.'

Joe put down his brandy.

'But my dear Harry, you don't mean to say that what you're really doing is to invent some sort of pill thing on which we've all got to live?'

'No, no, no. Nothing like that,' said Harry, laughing.

'So I understood,' said Joe, 'from Isabella.'

Harry savoured his cigar, his brandy, and the fact that he knew Isabella was the Countess della Quercia and called her by that name to her aristocratic and decidedly beautiful face. He felt expansive. He stretched his legs and laughed again.

'As a matter of fact, I don't think any of us would talk about food pills and all that nonsense, not in these days. It's the sort of thing you read in books twenty years ago.'

'I daresay it is,' said Joe. 'It must be that time ago since I opened one.'

'Any book?' asked Harry, incredulously.

'Well, to be quite truthful, I did read detective stories until I came here. I did it to improve my spelling. I never could spell properly. Now I don't have to, because Isabella does it for me. Her command of the English language is quite extraordinary. And French. And German for that matter. A most literate woman. Yes, indeed: it is a cross she has to bear. She considers it an incomprehensible streak of vulgarity in herself and she'd get rid of it if she didn't earn her living by it. None of her really distinguished ancestors could read or write, you see. Poor Isabella. She has so many crosses. For instance, ice-cream. Do you like ice-cream, Harry?'

'Not much. Well, as I was saying about food pills,' Harry went on, and Joe sighed gently. Isabella and ice-cream. It would have made a perfect after-dinner conversation. Snobbery and food. No topics could be more suitable. There was that third one, thought Joe sipping his brandy. What was it? Ah, yes. Pornography. Lord Chesterfield said that he always introduced the topic when the port was served. But no, thought Joe, I would not have liked Lord Chesterfield. Few people did, after all.

Joe woke from his reverie to realize that his guest was talking.

'I beg your pardon,' he said. 'What were you saying?'

'About the pills,' said Harry, slightly aggrieved.

'Oh ... ah yes,' said Joe and recovered himself. 'I'm afraid my thoughts wandered. You reminded me that I hadn't taken my own pills this evening, but I'm enjoying myself so much I've decided that I won't need them. Do go on.'

Harry, flattered, did so:

'As I was saying, it's all part of the bunkum they used to talk. Pills. Babies in bottles and robots that think. God knows what other tomfoolery. You see, it used to be a physicist's world. When you said "science" you meant physics. And in my opinion all physicists are bullies. They want to kick things around into shape. Their shapes. They'd like to mark off the universe like an army cantonment – all straight gravel paths, white-washed borders, and bull-shit. You follow me?'

Joe closed his eyes and sniffed his brandy. 'I limp along behind,' he said, 'but full of eagerness to learn.' He reflected that it was nothing less than the truth. For all his unfortunate after-dinner vocabulary, Harry had an original mind.

'Well, they've had their day,' said Harry, with a violent gesture that sent the ash of his cigar scattering over his clothes. 'It's been a long, long day, but it's nearly over. Now its the turn of the biologists, or it very soon will be. I admit we're not quite ready. More, I'll admit we're as far off beam as we may be. But it sometimes seems to me, when I read of what we're doing in the scientific journals, that – well – it's like what it was before Copernicus. There were lots of very intelligent men spending their lives working out just how many spheres of fixed stars there were, and just what loops the planets looped when they went round the earth, and just how big was the orbit of the sun – all very clever, very brainy, very painstaking stuff. Then comes along this man who looks at their results and says, "Ah, yes. Fine. But the earth goes round the sun." ' Harry paused and dusted the ash off himself, slapping and banging his clothes as though the ash were ants. He looked up sharply. 'Do you know,' he said, with a suddenly confidential tone, 'I used to think I might be the new Copernicus.'

'And well you might be,' said Joe. 'You're already a famous young man.'

'Thanks, but it won't do. Old Tommo says I'm finished and Tommo is never wrong.'

'Who,' said Joe, 'is Tommo?'

'Sir Gregory Thompson, F.R.S. We all call him Tommo. He likes it. Tommo said to me that I'd had one good idea and I was too old to have another. And that one idea isn't good enough. Not to make me a second Copernicus, at any rate. Tommo saw that, and I accept his verdict.'

Joe shook his head.

'In my opinion,' he said, 'for what it's worth, any distinguished man who actually *likes* people to call him Tommo has a streak of brashness in his nature. I'm sure his verdict was hasty, and wrong. By the way, what was the idea you had? That is, if you think I can possibly understand it.'

'It wasn't very complicated really,' said Harry. 'You see, like lots of other people, I work with desoxyribonucleic acid.'

'Ah,' said Joe, with a little gasp. 'I must remember that.'

'Call it DNA, like we all do.'

'No,' said Joe, firmly. 'I cannot bear this modern fad for initials. I find it much more confusing to remember them than the real words. You must write yours down on a slip of paper for me. Tomorrow. Well, you work with this acid. And then?'

'Well, there's a chap who made it in the laboratory, but I took the real stuff and tarted it up a bit. It's the thing which makes the chemistry of every living thing tick over. I put it into cells and the cells divide, and my stuff helps them do it. It's helping up there in that fig tree now.'

Joe looked up in wonder.

'You mean your,' he hesitated, 'stuff,' he said, and hesitated again, '*once you have tarted it up*,' he said, as though he were proudly using the first phrase he had learned in Mandarin Chinese, 'actually changes the working of the cells. How?'

'That,' said Harry, slapping his knee, 'is a damned fine question. The jackpot question as old Tommo would say.'

'I knew he was vulgar,' murmured Joe, but Harry in his enthusiasm did not hear him.

'The answer to it is that I don't know and I'm pretty sure I never shall. I know *what* it does. It makes the fruit of that tree big enough to knock your eye out. That's what I got my putty medal for.'

'Putty *what*?'

'The Nobel Prize,' explained Harry. 'Do you know, when I go to Salerno I put my specimen under that microscope. It's almost never working right. None of them does. But sometimes I'm lucky and I can get one picture. And in that picture I can just glimpse the actual molecule of the stuff. Shall we ever see into *that*: see its works – the actual works that are wound up to make a living thing? Well, maybe, one day. But we all know – those of us who aren't punch-drunk from the physicists, that is – we all know what we shall discover about the secret of life.'

'What?' asked Joe, holding his breath.

'Sweet F.A.,' said Harry.

'F.A.,' Joe repeated. 'Is that another acid?'

'F.A. Fanny Adams. Sweet Fanny Adams,' said Harry, half-exasperated and half-laughing. 'It's slang for 'nothing'. Nothing whatever. Not a single sausage.'

'Sausage,' repeated Joe, in awe. He was now thoroughly, but happily, at sea. 'Why?'

'Well,' said Harry. 'Take the physics boys. *Everything can be measured*, they said. And what happened? They did fine, measuring away and putting everything down neat and tidy in figures, until they came to measure electrons. They're the smallest thing we know. In fact, they're so small that we're not sure they *are* anything. They're probably just a sort of dimple in a field of force. As for me, I always think of them as the smile on the face of a Cheshire cat, because they've certainly got a high old sense of humour. Every time you try to measure them, you can't. They're not where they were when you started to measure them, and for why? Because you've tried to measure them, that's why. It's known as the Principle of Indeterminacy, and more familiarly the Bloody Spanner in the Works. Ever since it was discovered physicists have been trying to prove that it didn't exist, or if it did, it didn't matter. But it does matter.'

'I'm sure it does,' said Joe. 'But I'm not really sure that I understand it. Electrons, you say . . .' said Joe, frowning with mental effort.

'Look,' said Harry. 'Take snooker balls.'

'Oh no, please,' said Joe with dismay. 'Don't let's take snooker balls. I have a friend who tried for hours to teach me the game and I'm afraid I drove him quite desperate.'

'Not snooker balls, then,' said Harry amiably. He paused for a moment. He rather fancied his powers of explanation and he soon hit upon the right simile for his audience.

'Suppose,' he said, 'you were giving a dinner-party.'

'Ah!' said Joe, relaxing his expression. 'That's much better.'

'Suppose you asked twelve guests, but you had forgotten

you had only eleven seats at the table, even with a squeeze. Now, in they all troop and you begin sitting them down. Well, when you get to the twelfth man, somebody will stand up, won't they? – good manners and all that cock. Well, you sit *him* down and somebody *else* stands up: and so on and so on. You'll never get them seated, will you?'

'No,' said Joe, appreciatively. 'What a vivid picture you have drawn! I know some hostesses in Washington who are perfectly capable of doing a thing like that. What an excellent example, Harry. Now I understand perfectly about your principle of whatever it was. Yes, indeed. It's most clear. Only, of course, you really should never ask twelve people to a dinner-party. The rule to follow is "Less than the Muses and more than the Graces".'

Harry opened his mouth and then closed it again. 'I don't get it,' he said.

'Never mind if you don't,' said Joe. 'It's of no importance. Nobody gives dinner-parties like that any more. But what *you* were saying was of the greatest importance. Let us get back to Fanny Adams.'

'Who?' said Harry. Then, laughing, he said, 'I see what you mean. Now I think we biologists have got our own principle. It's the Principle of Negative Results, or, as I call it, "Now Look What You've Gone and Done, Clumsy".'

'How delightfully racy,' said Joe. 'I think I can almost guess what you mean.'

'Try,' said Harry.

'Well,' said Joe, barely noting that he was for once making a mental effort. 'I imagine that you mean that when you look inside that thingummy, you can see with that what d'you call it . . .'

'Microscope,' prompted Harry.

'Yes, that's it. Well, when you can see what that's made of, it will – to adopt your admirable scientific terminology – it will come to bits in your 'ands.'

'Bravo!' said Harry. 'That's an excellent description.'

'It *is*?' said Joe, glowing. 'You mean I have actually understood what you've been trying to tell me?' When Harry nodded, Joe went on, 'I am so very pleased. That's the first time it's happened with anybody for thirty years. You are certainly good company for a man like me.'

'It's not the whole story,' said Harry, 'but you've got the right end of the stick. When we can look inside the molecule, we may very well be able to take it apart. We might even put one together in the laboratory. But it won't be alive. We won't be able to make a jelly out of the contents of some bottles and then watch it crawl off the lab. bench.'

'Such a horrid thought. It reminds me of those dreadful jokes about cheeses that some people make, like having to buy a collar and chain.'

Harry guffawed briefly, but recovered himself. 'And the reason,' he went on, 'that we won't be able to do it is that a living thing is alive because – and only because – it is the direct descendant of the first living things that were made millions of years ago and which took millions of years of delicate interchanges and fine adjustments to get itself born. We can put the parts together, maybe, but we shall be like a child trying to put the pieces of a chronometer together in a tearing hurry before Papa comes in and finds out he's dropped it.'

Joe suddenly got to his feet in great excitement. He took a turn about the terrace on his short legs, saying, 'But ... but ... just a moment ... just a moment.' Then he stopped in front of Harry's chair and, almost unable to control his voice, said:

'But there's a better simile than that. And wonderful to say, I have thought of it. I, poor old stupid Joe.'

'What is it?' said Harry, dubiously.

'A *sauce*. There are some sauces – no, no, listen to me, please, Harry, or I shall forget the whole thing and that would be a personal tragedy. It's the first idea I have had in a quarter of a century. There are some sauces, Harry, that take seven hours to make. Now, when my cook first came here, he thought he would be very clever. He used all the right ingredients, but turned up the gas. He made the sauce in an hour and spent the spare time playing cards. I will not harrow you, on such a lovely night as this, with a description of what his sauce tasted like. Nor will I tell you of the agony of mind I went through, wondering what could be wrong, until Isabella came and solved the whole mystery. But you see – you do see, don't you? – that the sauce needed time, just like your jelly or whatever it was.'

'I do declare as my name's Harry Wesley that it is a better simile,' said Harry, generously.

'Oh, oh, oh,' said Joe, rocking on the balls of his feet. 'If only Oom Paul could be here now and hear poor old Joe being positively brilliant!'

'I can improve on it,' said Harry.

'You can?' Joe was, for a moment, crestfallen. 'Well, but I mustn't mind that, must I? All good ideas can be improved on. But the real thing is that the original one was mine.'

'My work is like your cook adding something special of his own. He doesn't change the sauce. He just helps the taste to develop. That's what I'm doing up there. I help the tree. I don't change it. I help it to do better. That's why I say we're never going to have machines that think, or babies in bottles or any of that nonsense. We're going to have to be much more modest. We're just going to help things to be richer and healthier. More modest, but more exciting, or so I think. I mean, just consider the problems it's going to solve. War, for instance. People make war to take things away from other people who've got something they want. But if you can grow as big figs as you like in your own back garden, you're not going to take the trouble of climbing over the fence and getting your trousers torn to pinch the man's next door. Are you?'

'What?' asked Joe, dreamily. 'Eh? Oh, I beg your pardon. I was thinking about my own simile ...' He coughed and remembered himself. 'Figs, you were saying.'

'Yes,' said Harry. But he, too, was dreaming. He looked into the reflection of the moon on the sea in front of them and thought of the statue to the saviour of mankind. He knew he wouldn't get one. He'd be forgotten as soon as the next man came up with an idea. But it was still pleasant to imagine the scene as it might have been.

Joe sat down and the two men were silent for a while. Far away down the coast little jets of coloured fire rose in the sky and fell scattering into the sea as some villagers let off fireworks in honour of a saint.

'Are they going to be very big figs?' asked Joe, at last.

'Enormous.'

'What will they taste like?'

'Can't say. Wonderful, I should imagine. I've never worked with figs before, and I wouldn't be doing it now if they hadn't told me the thing had to be done on a shoe-string. No money for extended tests. No money seems to be the trouble with everything here in Italy. Funny, when you come to think of all that money going up in smoke there.'

'You're not a religious man, then?'

'No. If I want superstition, I've only got to stick to science. The amount of superstition and sheer hocus-pocus that goes on in that would never be believed by anyone outside the racket. But I mustn't get on to that, or I'll be here all night.' He rose. 'Yes. They ought to be very tasty figs. I've eaten most of my other tests. Tomatoes. They simply melted in your mouth.'

Joe licked his lips.

'But they only had half doses. I'm trying a stronger treatment here because they've dinned into my head that for all the money they're spending – *all* – ha! – they want something commercial.'

The two men moved across the loggia and made their way to the gate of the garden.

'Harry,' said Joe. 'May I venture to ask you for a favour?'

'Of course.'

'Could I, do you think, taste one of your figs?'

Harry hesitated. Then he thought of the dinners, the wines, the cigars, and the company that Joe had given him.

'Certainly,' he said. 'I promise you some of the very first crop.'

*

The first fruits of any fig tree on the coast were known to be the best. But the first fruits of Harry's fig tree were so huge that Harry raised the height of his fences and double-locked the gate.

When the figs went on growing bigger, he put canvas screens round the wire-netting, doing the work himself so that no one should get a close view of the wondrous fruit. Harry did not know that his neighbours had put him down as an excise officer, but he did know that they were farmers. Even in England he had learned the unwisdom of showing his monster fruit to nearby farmers. By a rural logic which Harry never understood, they always argued, not that his experiments were making his own fruit grow bigger, but that they were stopping his neighbours' from growing just as big. He, therefore, kept his tree as secret as he could. Not even the foundling girl who looked after his house was allowed, any more, to peep.

When he judged the figs to be mature – and this he did by eye, by test-tubes, by microscopic slides, and by electrical measurements from hair-fine wires sunk into the fruit – he picked one of them. The twig from which he took the fig was carefully labelled with a plastic, weatherproof slip, on which Harry wrote in his clear, round hand, '*Removed for flavour by Wesley,'* and he followed this by the day and the hour in which the fruit was gathered. He then went into his laboratory, sat on a stool, peeled the magnificent fig with his penknife and slowly ate it.

He had no palate for figs. The taste was, for him, heavy, and a little like a purgative. But it was wholesome and the fruit was sound. He remembered his promise to Joe, and wondered how many it would be correct to send him. He did not wish to appear mean and send too few. On the other hand, the tree was a scientific experiment. He did not wish to strip it for the sake of mere good manners. He made up his mind to send six. To satisfy his conscience, Harry decided to wait a day or two before picking them, so that he could be quite sure that he had subjected them to all possible tests: then he could tell himself, truthfully, that if they continued to hang on the tree, that they would only rot.

*

Down in the house below, on the same morning, Joe complained that he had lost his appetite. He explained his worry at length to his anxious butler. He could no longer see Harry's figs because of the screens. But he was sure that Harry, in his ignorance of the finer points of gastronomy, was allowing the fruit to grow too ripe. The first crop of figs was the best, but only, Joe explained almost tearfully, if they were gathered on exactly the right day – almost, he had been told by experienced growers, on the exactly right hour. It would be pushing and rude to tell Harry, but Joe felt that if he were kept waiting much longer he would be constrained to do so. He refused to take any interest in luncheon, and ate almost nothing.

At sundown his butler, using a silver plate for the occasion, brought his master one gargantuan specimen of Harry's figs.

Joe looked at it with eyes as round as the plate it lay on.

'From Signor Wesley?' he asked.

The butler said that it wasn't. The butler said that it was a present from the foundling girl who looked after the English gentleman. It had fallen, he said, into her hand when she happened to be under the tree.

'You didn't *bribe* her, did you?' asked Joe.

The butler, having already arranged to have the thousand lire he had tipped the girl distributed through the next day's market bills, said, with indignation, that he hadn't.

Joe peeled the fruit with a silver knife. He placed a piece of it in his mouth with a silver fork. He savoured it. He ate it. Then two tears gathered in his eyes and tumbled down his round, red cheeks.

'This is how things tasted to Adam,' he said, solemnly, 'before Eve introduced him to ignobler pleasures and spoiled his palate for ever more.'

It was a remark he had made before on high gastronomic occasions, and he thought well of it. It could scarcely, however, have been more ill-chosen.

PART THREE

A⊤ half past three in the morning Joe woke up on the floor beside his bed, clutching his bolster to his chest. The bedsheets and cover were in disorder. The curtains between the pillars of the bed (for Joe indulged himself in a four-poster) were torn from their usual graceful folds and hung, bedraggled, half-off their curtain rings. The bed looked as though it had been the scene of some contest.

So, in a sense, it had. But Joe had been the only real protagonist. The other had been a naked woman of the most voluptuous shape who had planted dream kisses on Joe in an expert and shameful manner. Joe, shocked even in his dreams, had struggled to release himself from her embraces. He had put up a gallant fight – as the bed-curtains bore witness – but to his intense disgust had been, as it were, tripped up by his own body, and had been forced to yield. He distinctly remembered how they had fallen on the floor, locked inextricably together, and had found the carpet magically transformed into a mattress of swansdown.

Joe had never had such a dream before. He had nightmares, of course, especially when he had overeaten. But in these he was invariably a rather fat poodle who had stolen a string of sausages from a butcher and was chased by a policeman. In fact, all his dreams, both pleasant and alarming, had been about eating. But there had been nothing about food in this dream. There had been biting – Joe blushed to recall it – but no eating.

He got up from the floor, gave the bolster a disgusted kick, and went to the bathroom where he mixed himself a strong dose of bicarbonate of soda. He rearranged his bed as best he could in his amateur way, lay down, and soon fell asleep.

33

The dream came back. The bicarbonate had made no difference at all, except that the sylph or succubus or whatever it was, now lay on top of him instead of in his arms. His dream resistance was shorter this time, his yielding more abandoned. When he woke up, he turned on every light in the room and sat up until the dawn.

*

He barely touched his breakfast, and his staff, fearing a bad day, went about on tip-toe. He took a swim and lay in the sun. He placed a pair of opaque spectacles over his eyes, specially moulded to his features in a light plastic. They brought darkness and the woman again, this time accompanied by three companions, without a stitch of clothing or a modest idea among them. After weakly allowing them all to kiss him, Joe threw off his spectacles in a rage. The four beauties disappeared slowly in a green and purple light.

Joe ate no luncheon. His cook burst into tears and told his wife to prepare to sell the jewellery which he had bought her over the years from overcharges on the daily account. As for Joe, he took a sedative and went to bed. The sedative sent him to sleep, but also loosened what ever little moral restraint he might have had over his sleeping self. He woke at five, heavy-eyed. He ate a mouthful or two at dinner to calm his butler, who was a prey to such nerves that the neck of the bottle clattered against the glass as he poured his master's wine. He, poor man, had no wife, and the money from his own embezzlements had all gone on horses.

When the meal was over he ventured to ask his master if he had had bad news.

'No,' said Joe. Then he said, 'Minu, you're a bachelor, aren't you?'

'Yes, signor,' said Minu, aloud, and to himself, 'Sant' Andrea, please don't let it be the horses. I'll pay him back, I swear I will.'

'Minu,' said Joe, 'do you have bad dreams?'

'What sort, *signor?*'

'About women – beautiful, dangerous women.'

Minu, relieved at the turn of the conversation, hugely relaxed. Grinning, he said, 'I call those good dreams, not bad.'

The expression on his master's face caused Minu such a fright that he ended on a squeak.

'Do you have them?' said Joe. 'That's what I asked.'

'Sometimes,' said Minu, whispering, to be sure of his timbre. 'At least I used to.'

'Not any longer?'

'No, *signor.*'

'Why?'

'If you will excuse the phrase, *signor*, because I go to bed drunk.'

'Of course, of course, of *course*,' said Joe, half to himself. He smiled for the first time that day. 'A splendid idea. I should have thought of it myself. Minu,' he said, turning to his butler, 'this is a day of celebration for me. It's ... it's ... it's the anniversary of my coming to Italy. Minu, do me the honour of bringing a bottle of brandy and getting drunk with me tonight.'

Three hours later, Minu helped his master to bed, tucked him up, and went to tell the others in the kitchen to quieten the roistering which had broken out when he had tipped them the wink that the old devil wasn't going to sack the lot of them, but was just having nightmares.

For the first three hours of the night Joe slept, as he had always done, like a child. At half past two the women arrived, vine decked, with three male lovers, hairy and bronzed men who challenged Joe to contests of love. He woke with the coming of daylight. It had been worse than ever. The previous night they had at least been lying down. Joe, shuddering at the thought, had never before believed that people made love on their feet.

Next morning, when he went to shave, he looked nervously in the mirror, expecting to see a leer on his face. What he did see caused him such a surprise that he switched on all the lights and looked again. The curl of hair that usually lay flat across the top of his balding head, stood up, like a baby's coxcomb. His cheeks shone with health. His eyes were clear; their expression was crisp and happy. He looked for a full minute and decided that he had not been mistaken at his first glance. He was not saturnine: he was cherubic.

*

At ten o'clock that same morning Isabella locked the door of her small house behind her, and set out along the coast road towards Joe Bellman's villa. She remembered that it was the first of the month. Among the cheques that she would write out for Bellman's signature would be one for her own honorarium. It would not be large: she had refused to accept anything that smelt of charity. But it would pay her rent. That would be one good thing about the day. It was not likely that there would be any others. The sky was leaden, the sea an oily grey, and the sirocco was blowing. When the sirocco blew she felt the weight of her ancestry particularly heavy upon her.

It was a great burden at all times. The blood of the della Quercias ran in her veins: rather too much of it, for she was convinced that she was descended from the brother and sister, who, famously, were incestuous and had a child. Then there was the della Quercia cunning, the della Quercia guile, the della Quercia treachery, and the della Quercia fondness for poisoning their enemies. In the Renaissance, these traits had carved out for them a rich patrimony in the Papal States. But it was a grim inheritance, thought Isabella, as she walked along the road, for one twenty-eight-year-old unmarried woman to bear alone.

The other della Quercias had given up trying. At a suitable time after the war they had sold up every palace and acre they had and put their money into the ice-cream business. Like so many industrial ventures at that time in Italy, it had been enormously successful. *Quercias* – an ice-cream on a stick – were eaten throughout Italy. The family that once poisoned a cardinal now printed certificates of hygiene on paper cups of an ice-cream called 'For Baby'. The patrons of Bramante and the Caracci brothers, of Caravaggio and Bernini, covered Italy with posters so hideous that the intelligent part of the public, fearful for the tourist trade, had risen in outrage. The posters had come down, for a while, but they came back. Isabella passed one now and averted her eyes. It showed a family of children with their mother looking anxiously out of the window. The legend ran, 'Drive carefully, Father: they are waiting for you. And don't forget to take them back a *Quercia*.' The della Quercia guile that had once set a pope rolling on the floor and biting the carpet in wild anger had come to this. As for the della Quercias, they all enjoyed their change of fortune immensely. They dropped the prefix to their names, they swore they were all descended from a pontifical pastry cook, and they rejoiced when their children instead of developing the thin della Quercia noses, the della Quercia smile, were fat, bouncing, and thoroughly bourgeois, a result not only of three meals a day but of the fact that the della Quercias had married into the mineral water business.

Isabella had refused to touch a penny of their money. They had thought her quaint, but secretly they admired her and saw to it, privately, that she did not starve. She employed her gifts in translating books, one of them an enormous history of the della Quercia family written by a nineteenth-century German in eight thick volumes. It was a work no sane publisher would ordinarily touch; but one publisher, fortified by ice-cream and mineral water, agreed to take the risk. Isabella, therefore, ate. Not much, it was true, but enough. The other Quercia women admired the way she kept her figure. Indeed, anyone seeing her as she walked along the coast road, tall, dark-eyed, and with that fine moulding of the forehead and the chin that one sees in the famous Florentine portraits of the della Quercia women, would have put her down as a remarkably handsome woman.

She, for her part, later that morning and for the first time in her life, put Joe down as a handsome man. She told herself that the thing was absurd. He was no thinner, his head was as round, his nose as buttonish, and he was still parboiled. But he had come in, unusually, to watch her sort out his letters. He had greeted her with *empressement* – again a most unusual thing, since he was a man who was shy in his necessary formalities. She had at once noticed a change in him. There was an aura, she thought, a male aura, a sort of masculine effulgence which made him seem like a rich American in the travel magazines, at home in his Californian villa. She noticed how firm his flesh was for a man who must be fifty. He smelt nice, she thought. She wondered why nobody had married him. She thought it might be nice to marry him herself and raise a family. But at this point she caught herself up. She had forgotten for the first time in many years, the fateful curse of the della Quercia blood. It must be, she decided that the sirocco had lifted.

'You mustn't mind if I seem a bit ... a bit ... strange,' said Joe. 'It's the south wind blowing, I think. Do you ... would you mind if I come and sit beside you at the desk?'

'Certainly not, Joe. It's your desk. And a very nice desk, too. What is it? Directoire?'

'I think so,' said Joe, uneasily. 'At any rate it ...' He paused. He swallowed. He plunged. 'It never looks so nice as when a lovely woman like you is sitting at it.' Having blurted this sentence at her, he rapidly took a handkerchief from his pocket and swabbed his forehead.

Then he groaned, 'Oh, my God, Isabella. What have I said? But what have I said?'

'Nothing so very dreadful,' Isabella replied. 'You paid me a compliment.'

'I know,' said Joe, miserably. 'I do hope you won't think it showed any lack of respect for you.'

He looked so comically dismayed that Isabella laughed. She pursed her lips primly, folded her hands over her stomach and said in the accents of a genteel English housekeeper, 'Oh, Mr Bellman, Ay am sure Ay know my place and no offence is taken where none was meant, sir.' This made Joe even more miserable, so, laughing again, she said, 'Joe, you certainly are odd, this morning. I think it really must be the sirocco. Here,' she said, pulling up a chair, 'come and sit beside me and watch me save you hundreds and hundreds of dollars.'

Joe slid on to the chair so swiftly that Isabella gave a little jump. He shifted the chair closer so that their knees were touching. It was charming, it was gallant, but he insisted on spoiling it by muttering a string of fierce apologies.

'Well, now,' she said, taking up a letter, 'what have we here?'

Joe bubbled over with words. 'Yes. That one. That's it. That's the letter I wanted to discuss with you. It's been worrying me. It came last night. I couldn't sleep. At least I did sleep, worse luck: I mean ... well,' he ended, his voice rising in desperation, 'You can see how worried I am.'

'But this is just a letter from the Ministry saying you must pull down your east loggia because it was built without the inspector approving the design.'

'Exactly!' said Joe. He edged even closer to her. He put his hand on hers. He squeezed it. He should, to have completed the approach, have said something flippant, or pointless, and smiled. Instead, with an expression of the deepest alarm, he said urgently:

39

'Pull it down! Don't you see how terrible that would be? All the workmen in the house. The cost of it . . .'

'But Joe, I've already told you. It's all settled. I'm going to bribe the inspector with five hundred dollars of your money, and there'll be no trouble at all.'

'But . . .' said Joe. He pecked at her shoulder with his lips. 'But there's nothing in writing. Is there? Is there, Isabella? Oh, do say something quickly. Anything, but say something.'

'You know I've talked to him. Joe. He's a very decent fellow. He can't very well write anything down, but he did say to me that so far as he is concerned for five hundred dollars you can build a Mohammedan mosque for all he cares and he'll approve the design.'

'Mohammedan,' repeated Joe, staring at her. 'I'm worse than any Mohammedan. Another night like last night and I shall be rollicking with concubines at ten in the morning. I can't stand it, Isabella. I'm a good man, a sober man, a clean-minded man, a man who keeps himself to himself. Just look,' he said, suddenly, 'what I'm doing with my hands.'

She did not need to look, because he was stroking her breasts through her frock: expertly, she thought.

'Isabella,' said Joe. 'Isabella, I'm going to kiss you.'

He kissed her lingeringly. It was an excellent kiss, a beguiling kiss, a kiss of a passionate and experienced lover.

Joe took his lips away. He got up. Tears of remorse were running down his cheeks. 'I'm so very, very sorry. Please do say you believe me when I tell you it's the sirocco.'

'Joe,' she replied, 'am I so unattractive that I have to believe it needs a hot wind blowing from Libya to make a man kiss me?'

'No,' said Joe, humbly. 'You're very beautiful. I never knew before how beautiful you are.' She got up and went towards him. Joe, struggling briefly with himself, took her in his arms.

The butler, Minu, catching sight of them through the shutters some ten minutes later as they lay together on a couch, made off immediately to the servants' quarters. Flinging open the door of the kitchen, which was filled with servants busily preparing lunch, he struck an operatic pose.

He delivered his welcome news as an impromptu aria: 'Good friends and dear companions,' he sang, 'it was love, it was love, it was love.' Then, his voice cracking and his invention giving out, he ended in his speaking voice: 'The old buzzard's got the Countess on the couch. That was what was troubling him, the goat.' Everybody in the kitchen heaved a great sigh of relief.

*

'We shall be seen,' said Isabella, holding Joe away from her, but gently. 'Let us go to your bedroom.'

'Never!' said Joe, passionately. 'That horrible place makes me think of nothing but sex.'

Isabella thought that in the circumstances the remark was strange, especially since Joe accompanied it with a rain of kisses. She reflected, in such time as she had at her disposal, that Joe was an American, and she had observed that they were a people who needed high moral thoughts as other men need liquor. It stimulated them in war; perhaps it stimulated them in bed.

'All the same,' said Joe, miserably, 'you're right. We shall be caught and I shall lose my cook's respect. Let us go to the blue guest-room. Do you know where it is?'

'The one across the corridor?'

'Yes. Let's go there.'

'Yes,' said Isabella. Then, as Joe did not release her from his empassioned hug, she said: 'But to do that, Joe, you must let me get up.'

'Eh?' said Joe. 'Oh! Yes, of course. I'm sorry.' He got to

41

his feet. 'I – that is – I suppose I should lead the way,' he said, with a helpless little gesture.

'No, Joe,' said Isabella, 'we're not going in to dinner.'

'That's true,' said Joe, 'we're certainly not,' and never did a man sound more forlorn.

She went to the blue guest-room and began to take off her clothes. Joe followed her after a few moments. When he had closed and locked the door, he began to strip off his clothes with the haste and modesty of a man preparing for an impromptu swim in a river, fearful of being observed in the nude. He jumped into the bed and sat up, pulling the sheet under his chin. His curl of hair stood up, his cheeks shone, and he looked more babyish than ever. He also looked, thought Isabella, a most attractive man.

They made love. When she could no longer see the expression of profound dismay in her lover's eyes, Isabella found him most satisfactory. His gallantry was prolonged and enterprising, his passion surprised her. It flabbergasted Joe.

After a while, they lay quietly side by side in the large bed : or rather, they lay parallel, for as soon as his love-making was over, Joe had moved away to the edge of the bed.

In spite of the tumult of his feelings, Joe could not resist asking a natural question.

'Isabella.'

'Yes, Joe.'

'I know I've disgraced myself in your eyes for ever, but ... well ...'

'Well, what, Joe?'

'Have I disgraced myself, if you know what I mean? Have I disgraced myself in the ... in the ...?'

'In the wars, Joe?'

'Yes.'

'You've covered yourself with glory.'

'Well, that's something, at any rate,' said Joe. Then he made a noise between a sigh and a groan.

'Do you know what you reminded me of when you made love, Joe?'

'An escaped lunatic?'

'Not at all. You were like a Hindu who had been forced to eat beef and to his horror discovered he liked the taste of the stuff.'

'The poor, poor devil,' said Joe. 'How I feel for him.' He turned her description over in his mind and thought how well it fitted him. But what had forced *him* to eat, so to speak, his beef? What had got into his blood so suddenly?

'I'm hungry,' he said, at length.

'So am I,' said Isabella.

'What's the time, Isabella?'

She looked at the clock on the table on her side of the bed. 'Eleven.'

'Two hours to lunch,' said Joe, gloomily.

'Couldn't we ask Minu to ask the cook to get us something now?'

'At *eleven*,' said Joe, shocked. 'My dear Isabella, that is the sort of awful thing they do on ships. Ox-tail soup,' he said, and shuddered. 'I've never had a snack in my life.'

'Then let's have some champagne,' said Isabella. 'Wouldn't that be nice?'

'Well,' said Joe, doubtfully, 'I don't know. I've never drunk champagne in the morning. It's the sort of thing actresses are supposed to do, isn't it?'

'And fast women,' said Isabella.

'Yes.'

Isabella stretched her arms luxuriously over her head.

'Well, what am I,' she asked, 'but a fast woman? You've made me one, you wicked man, this very morning. I am ruined, Joe, and you've done it. I shall not only have champagne, but caviare. And thank your lucky stars I don't want lobster mayonnaise into the bargain.'

'Oh dear,' said Joe. 'Don't joke about it, please. I shall

write you a letter of apology explaining everything. When, that's to say, I know what the explanation is.'

With that he got up, put on his clothes and, carefully closing the door behind him, went in search of Minu.

They had their champagne and Isabella her caviare on the end terrace. Minu had laid a small marble table and for a centre-piece he had used a basket of fruit. On top of the fruit were four ripe figs, the ordinary figs of the coast.

Joe did not see them at first, because he was looking out at the view to avoid the embarrassment of catching Isabella's eye. But when the champagne was poured, he turned towards her, and saw the figs.

He went green in the face, set his glass down on the marble table so forcibly that the foot cracked. He ordered Minu to take the fruit away.

'Is there anything wrong with it, *signor*?' asked Minu, anxiously.

'Yes. No. I don't know,' said Joe. 'I'm not feeling well, I think. I can't tell what's wrong with me.'

'I'm sorry sir,' said Minu, and went away hastily with the basket.

But for the first time in two days, Joe did know what was wrong with him, or at least he guessed. He made up his mind to see Harry as soon as he could.

*

But Harry had gone to Salerno, in great haste. On the way he had left a letter for Isabella at her house, marked both front and back with the word 'urgent'. She did not get it until that evening. The two hours to luncheon had passed quickly, for Joe, once the fruit had been removed, recovered his spirits and his confidence in himself. He set out to entertain Isabella as though nothing unusual had happened, and he succeeded; although at times he fell silent, or took sidelong glances at her, or drummed with his fingers on the arm of the chair. The meal had been the cook's best, but Joe's appetite had gone once more and he ate little of it.

Isabella, on the other hand, had eaten well. She was a happy woman. She had a lover, and she was proud of it. She had no conscience about such things, she told herself. After all, the blood of the della Quercias ran in her veins: and Joe was not even her brother or her sister's husband: he was not even a cousin. A man whose father had been hanged for murder committed in an access of rage will not feel unduly put out if he loses his temper and punches someone on the nose. After all, the Isabella della Quercia, after whom she had been named, threw her lover into a dungeon and had him strangled. Isabella stole a glance at Joe, with his upright curl and round baby face. She had decided that she never could throw him into a dungeon. She might, at the most, spank him.

*

Back once more in her own small house, Isabella opened Harry's note. It had been typed in a great haste. It began with several apologies for troubling her and then went on to say that Harry needed a notice to put up on his wire fences in case someone should try and steal the fruit on his tree. It would be quite a feat, wrote Harry, but he had heard that Neapolitan thieves were very agile. So he wanted a warning notice, which he would illuminate at night, and the notice should be in the sort of Italian that anybody would understand. His own was too bookish he thought. The notice must say, in plain language, that the fruit on the tree had been chemically treated. If eaten, the chemical might have an effect upon certain people. Harry had been most uncertain about how the effect should be described, because he had typed 'dangerous', crossed it out, typed 'unpleasant', crossed this out, written 'unsettling', crossed this out vigorously in blue crayon, and had finally written 'deleterious'.

She smiled. It was a very English word, as English as Harry

himself. It was as misty, as full of nuances as an English September morning. There would be nothing in Italian like it. She took up the dictionary and knew she would find a list of words, all rolling off the tongue like honey, and each of them brutally plain in their meaning. There they were, just as she expected: *velenoso, distruttivo, micidiale*. They seemed to hum the tune they should be sung to. They were all quite clear. But did Harry mean his figs were poisonous? or destructive? or deadly?

She sat slowly down at her work-table and took up her pencil. Her thoughts ran for a moment on the few months she had spent teaching at an English school for girls, a job the della Quercias had quietly found for her. She had been made much of because of her title for a while. But then one of the girls who did not like her had asked, with as much insolence as she dared, for a translation of 'Mind your own business'. Months of prunes and prisms and English decorum had worn away Isabella's tact. She felt she could not tell a lie.

'The phrase in Italian is *Fare i cazzi vostri*,' she had said. 'Fishermen sometimes use it as the name of their boats.' She had looked the impertinent girl straight in the eye – for she was sure the girl already knew the phrase – and she gave her the English translation. 'It means,' she had said, 'literally, "mind your own cock".'

For a while she had felt like the Condottiere della Quercia, who rides his horse with such proud disdain in the piazza at G—. Then she had been asked to resign.

She tried her best with Harry's notice for a while, but gave up. If Harry had put up the notice in England, she could imagine the English reading it, expressionless, and going away with a foggy notion of general alarm in which warning detonators – 'deadly', 'poisonous', 'destructive', for instance, would dully explode at intervals. And they would not touch the figs. But if she put anything so vague – supposing it could be done – in the clear light of the coast, she knew quite well what would happen. Her countrymen would read it, as they did every notice. Their curiosity would be fatally aroused, and they would not rest until they had stolen a fig and found out if the notice meant that they would be seized with stomach pains, or come out in spots, or be stretched out dead upon the ground.

'Warning!' she wrote, at last. 'These figs have been treated with medicine. If they are eaten, they may give some people a belly-ache. No thieving. Stay out. Cod. Civ. Pen. Sec. 32.' she added, with a flourish, warning the intending thief of the penalties of the law for thieving. She got a stamp from her desk drawer, stuck it on a sheet of paper to show the tax was paid (for she knew that this was something Harry would forget to do) and typed the message in capitals.

She sat back and admired her own sensible, helpful efficiency for a moment, and then her della Quercia gorge rose. She had taken three quarters of an hour over the trivial little job. One of her ancestors had overthrown the Signoria of T— in thirty minutes and made himself master of the town for life.

Then she said to herself:

'But never mind. Today I have had a lover.'

She felt very much better.

*

Isabella had done Harry an injustice. He knew with great precision why the figs should not be eaten. But it was the sort of reason that could not be put up publicly, not even in Italian. His visit to Salerno had confirmed his diagnosis of the trouble, and now, on his return, he was pacing up and down his small house distractedly.

It was in this state of mind that Isabella found him. The more she had thought about having a lover the better she had felt, until she decided that she could stay in the house no longer, but must take a walk. It was evening, and judging that Harry would be back, she put her notice in an envelope and made up her mind to deliver it herself. The walk along the upper road was beautiful; she would save Harry another journey, and besides, she had never seen inside his house.

Harry opened the door to her. When he saw who she was an expression of the greatest alarm crossed his face. Isabella, explaining her mission in order to fill in the silence, had the impression that at any moment he might close the door on her. She noticed that he was trembling and she wondered if perhaps he were ill.

But when, at last, he allowed her in and they stood face to face in his living-room, she saw that it was quite to the contrary. He was in magnificent health. The English pallor which he had maintained in spite of the sunshine had suddenly disappeared. He was bronzed, but not as though he had been in the sun. The colour seemed to come from within him, just as his drab hair now glowed with a light, it appeared, of its own. Nobody could ever have called Harry a good-looking man, yet, Isabella decided, there was an air of handsomeness about him that she had never noticed before.

Only his manner was left of the Harry she had known, and this had become exaggerated to an extraordinary degree. His awkwardness had become painful. He walked backwards into chairs, he blurted out answers to her questions, he forgot to ask her to sit down, and when she took a step towards him he retreated as though he were in mortal terror of her.

She was puzzled. She asked if she had interrupted his work, but he shook his head. Then she said that she would leave the notice and go.

At this Harry swallowed hard, blinked and pulled himself together. Knocking over a bottle in the process, he got out some wine and some olives from a cupboard and pressed her to sit down and drink with him. He drained one glass quickly and this seemed to still his nerves. He looked at Isabella for a long minute, saying nothing. Then he sighed deeply. It was, thought Isabella, marvelling at the way he was behaving, a distinctly languishing sigh.

She took out the notice and showed it him. He read it carefully. Then he laughed, a loud and unhumorous laugh.

'Belly-ache,' he said, and laughed again. 'Belly-ache.'

Isabella explained her difficulties.

'And then it's something that the boys will understand,' she said. 'After all, its boys who are most likely to try and climb your wire fences.'

'It's not boys I'm worried about,' said Harry. 'They'll be safe.' Then he suddenly put his hand to his mouth. 'Oh, my gawd,' he said. 'They might not be.' He stared at Isabella over his fingers with round frightened eyes.

'What do you mean, Harry?'

Harry took his hand away slowly.

'Never mind,' he said. He poured himself some more wine with a shaking hand, forgot to refill his guest's glass, remembered, and spilt wine on the table.

'Thanks a lot,' he said, 'for the notice. It's just right. I'll put it up in the morning.'

'Harry,' said Isabella. 'I don't want to be curious, but what is wrong with the figs? Or can't you tell me?'

'No,' said Harry, so abruptly that he almost shouted. Then, more quietly, 'No, Countess, I really can't tell you. Trade secret and all that rot. Look here,' he said, 'tell you what I can show you though. I can show you my lab. I don't suppose you've ever been in one, have you?'

When Isabella said she hadn't, Harry went on in a torrent of words to describe the apparatus in it. It was plain that she was being headed off.

She was taken into the small laboratory. She was shown various instruments that she did not understand and finally she was led to a bench on which stood three tall black and brass microscopes.

'That one there,' said Harry, 'with the double eye-piece is stereoscopic. I'll put a slide in it, and you can have a look. You've got equal sight, haven't you? Yes, of course you have,' he said, looking deep in her eyes with a most strange expression. 'Here. Look through there and see what you see.'

She bent over, adjusted the eyepieces, and stared at the coloured, translucent structure of a plant cell. 'It's wonderful, isn't it?' said Harry, behind her.

She felt Harry's hand on her seat. She continued to look through the microscope, hoping that Harry would regret what he was doing. He did not. She straightened up. She turned and faced him.

'It is *quite* wonderful,' she said sternly. 'It is like a landscape in a dream. Indeed, I would not have known that I was awake if you had not pinched my bottom.'

Harry flushed till the veins swelled on his forehead.

'I ... I ... don't know how I can explain ...' he said, hoarsely.

'I don't think it's necessary,' said Isabella. 'After all, this is the first time I have been in a scientific laboratory, and I don't know your manners and customs. For all I know it might be quite usual for you to pinch ...'

'Oh,' moaned Harry, 'please don't ...'

'Visitors' bottoms,' went on Isabella, as firmly as she had gone on with her translation in the girls' school. 'Like medical students, for instance,' she said. 'Everybody knows they have very free and easy ways.'

'I'm not a medical student,' said Harry. 'I'm just a ... rotter.' To Isabella's embarrassment, tears began to roll down his cheeks.

'And you ... you a countess,' he said, and sank down, frankly crying, on a stool.

He was so contrite that she could no longer be angry with him. She put her hand on his shoulder.

'My being a countess, Harry,' she said, 'makes it quite all right. It's not the first time a della Quercia's behind has been pinched.'

'Isn't it?' said Harry, sniffing loudly, and still crying.

'No,' said Isabella. 'Here, take your handkerchief and dry your eyes,' she said, pulling his handkerchief from his breast-pocket. Harry took it and blew his nose.

'The most famous time', said Isabella, 'was in 1482. It was Caterina della Quercia's bottom and the man who did it was the Holy Roman Emperor.'

'Honi soit qui mal y pense and all that,' said Harry, managing a trembling smile.

'Not quite,' said Isabella. 'He did it in public. Everybody could see what he had done. Caterina, with great presence of mind, turned round and smacked the face of the courtier standing next to her. The courtier bowed profoundly and withdrew. That's how we got our castle in F——. The Emperor was so pleased with Caterina that he gave it to her husband. Now, Harry,' she said, pushing back the hair off his forehead, 'do you feel better?'

Harry sniffed again, but if the description may be used, he sniffed rather more cheerfully.

'Well,' he said, drying his eyes. 'I do, a bit. But I daresay that Holy Roman Emperor did that to all the countesses he met. But you see, I'm not an emperor. I'm just Harry Roland Wesley, D.SC., and I've never in my life done anything like it. Never, Isabella. I do hope you'll believe me, though I can't for the life of me see why you should. I wish I could explain why I did it.'

'Perhaps I reminded you of a girl friend of yours back in England. She's probably always bending over microscopes and you're probably always ruining her experiments.'

'No,' said Harry. 'I haven't got a girl friend.'

'Then perhaps it was the wine. Yes, let's say it was our famous coastal wine.'

'No,' said Harry, 'I always water it before I put it in the decanter, and anyway I'm as sober as a judge.'

'Well,' said Isabella, with a touch of impatience in her voice, 'we'll say it was the sirocco.'

'Can't be,' said Harry. 'It stopped blowing at five and now the wind's in the north. I checked the anemometer just before you came.'

'Then, for God's sake, Harry,' said Isabella, raising her voice, 'let's say it was my bottom and be done with it.'

Harry cleared his throat. 'Logically . . .' he began.

'Oh!' said Isabella, sinking on a laboratory stool. 'The English!'

Harry blushed again. 'I'm afraid I'm not making out very well, Countess. I'm no good at this sort of thing. I think the only thing I can do is just say I'm sorry, but I don't really know how to do that,' he finished, tears threatening to flow again.

'Look,' said Isabella, firmly. 'If you were an Italian, do you know what you would do?'

'No, Countess.'

'You would look into my eyes and say, "Isabella, I do not apologize. You may smack my face; you may never speak to me again, but I shall never apologize. You are a beautiful woman. I am a man. Your posteriors are more exquisitely proportioned than those of the Venus Callipygos. They are of marble. I have tried to pinch them when nobody was looking. Yours are of flesh. I do not need to say anything more in my defence."'

'What's Callipygos mean?' asked Harry.

'Beautiful-bottomed,' said Isabella. 'It's a statue. Then I would pretend to draw my hand away, very slightly, but . . .'

'The beautiful-bottomed Venus,' said Harry. 'Well, I never. Where is it?'

'In the Vatican,' said Isabella, and Harry said, 'Coo, just think of that. In a place like . . .' but Isabella said loudly, 'Harry, shut up and listen to me.'

'Yes, mum,' said Harry, contritely.

'I would pretend,' Isabella went on, 'to withdraw my hand, but you would tighten your hold on it. I would yield. You would kiss my finger-tips, twice, and I would allow you to do so. You would know you had been forgiven. There. what do you think of that?'

'Very pretty,' said Harry.

'"Pretty" or "not-so-bad" or "could-be-worse" or "jolly, what?" or whatever you choose to call it,' said Isabella, with her best imitation of an English mutter, 'that's just what you're going to do.'

'Me? I couldn't.'

'You shall,' said Isabella. 'Forfeits. I insist. Now, come along, say it after me.'

Harry paid his forfeit as best he could through Isabella's laughter and, finally, when he came to kiss her hand, through his own. There, Isabella ended the matter.

But when he had seen her to the gate, bidden her good-bye, and watched her until she was out of sight, he said to himself, as he carefully double-locked the entrance:

'Still, I bet she thinks I'm a wolf. But I'm not. I'm a respectable man, so help me God.' He turned back to his house. He saw the fig-tree outlined against the late evening sky, and he shuddered. He opened the gate again and went for a brisk walk.

*

About a mile beyond Harry's house there was a promontory. It was a tall cliff and at its edge someone had made a public belvedere with a pine tree and stone seats that had been long neglected and were crumbling. The view from this place was the most magnificent in Southern Italy. It swept the whole of the Salerno Bay, from the far Calabrian coast, round past the town itself, along the cliffs where Harry and Joe lived, over the rocks at the foot of the cliff to a long stretch of coastline set out with houses with here and there a church, until, in the far distance, it ended with the Fara-glioni rocks of the island of Capri, just visible beyond the end of the peninsula.

Beautiful as the view was, the belvedere was almost always deserted, partly because Italians do not like exposed places, and partly because the steps that led up to it were tiring and dangerous since they had not been repaved for half a century.

But the climb was what Harry needed. Out of breath, but feeling both cleaner and calmer from the exercise, he reached the belvedere just as the fishing-boats with their great star-like lamps were setting out for the night. He sat on one of the benches and watched the boats congregate in groups that looked like towns and villages seen at night only by the light of their street lamps. One configuration reminded him of a hill in South London that he had seen for years as he made his way home on the dark winter evenings from school. Nos-talgia made him bite his lip for a moment to stop himself from crying again.

He thought of his dreams.

He thought of the fig tree.

He swore, aloud, in the still night air.

A voice said:

'Is that you, Harry?'

Harry looked landwards and saw a short, stumpy silhou-ette.

'Joe?'

'Yes.'

'I didn't know you ever came up as far as this,' said Harry, resentful at being disturbed.

'I don't usually. Only when I'm worried.' Joe came across the open space and leaned against the seaward wall near Harry's seat, looking at the fishing-boats below. The light of their lamps broadly reflected from the sea, lit his face and Harry's. He paused. 'Have you had a good day?'

'I've had a bloody day.'

'So have I,' said Joe. 'I've ... I've ... I've been seeing ...' He fell silent. Then, with the expression of a man who must tell someone of his troubles, he finished, 'I've been seeing Isabella.'

'So have I,' said Harry.

'I gave her lunch.'

'I pinched her bottom,' said Harry.

'Good heavens!'

'She was damned nice about it,' Harry went on. 'It runs in the family, it seems.'

'Harry,' said Joe, and he came and sat beside him. 'Surely you don't *usually* ...'

'You bet your life I don't.'

'Do you know what *I* did to Isabella?' said Joe, almost in a whisper.

'No.'

'Can you guess?'

'No.'

'Well, you've *got* to guess,' said Joe, protestingly. 'It's something I can't tell you.'

'Why?'

'Because it isn't done. Now do you know?'

'Haven't the foggiest notion,' said Harry.

'Oh, don't be so obtuse and *British*,' said Joe, stamping his foot.

'That's the second time today,' Harry began, and then trailed off. Suddenly he exclaimed:

'My God!' Then he stayed silent for a while. 'But how can it be possible?' he said aloud to himself. At length he turned to Joe. 'Isabella,' he said, heavily. 'So you made love to her.'

'Yes.'

'All the way?'

'Yes.'

'No wonder she took a mere pinch so calmly,' said Harry.

55

'She took everything calmly,' said Joe, 'but I can tell you frankly, I didn't, Harry. This morning I behaved like a drunken Don Juan. I didn't know I knew so much Harry, I was a great lover.'

'My congratulations,' said Harry.

'There is nothing to congratulate me about,' said Joe. 'It was quite horrible. What's more,' he said, tragically, 'I have been put off my food. And, forgive me for saying so, Harry, but I think it's your fault.'

'You do?' said Harry. 'Then forgive *me* for saying so, but have you been pinching my figs?'

'I was coming to that,' said Joe, with as much dignity as he could summon up. 'The girl who works for you was so kind as to send one down to my butler, who gave it to me.'

There was an ominous silence from Harry.

'She said it fell off into her hand,' finished Joe, weakly.

'I locked the place up,' said Harry. 'How did the little bitch get in?'

'Locks mean nothing to servants, Harry. You should know that.'

'I've never had a servant in my life.' Harry replied. 'But you're right. She must have slipped in when she called me away to sign a receipt for the postman. So much shrieking and hand-waving, there was, I didn't rightly know what I was doing.'

'Then it *is* the figs, Harry.'

'Did you eat yours?'

'Yes.'

'Every bit of it?'

'Yes.'

'Then if you've got the trouble, it *must* be the figs,' said Harry, sombrely. 'It must be. I've been thinking ever since it began with me. . . .'

'You mean those dreams and ... and ... well those dreams.'

'Yes: and the mixed-up yearning sort of feeling,' said Harry, and Joe shuddered. 'Well, when it began to happen, I guessed what might have gone wrong. But I thought it was some of the serum – the acid I told you about – that had got lost and got into my food. That nosey girl might have been poking around my laboratory. But when I was over in Salerno this morning I had already begun to suspect there was something else. Now I know.'

'But Harry, for heaven's sake, tell me what's happened. How long will it last? Is there a cure?' said Joe, desperately; and then with a wail, he said, 'Shall I never enjoy another meal in my whole life? Only women, women, women, women. No,' he said, brokenly. 'I can't bear to think of it.'

Harry sighed long and heavily.

'You see, Joe, it's like this. Or so I think. The stuff I used makes the tree – plant – bush – anything give better crops. Now one of the ways it works is through the reproductive organs. So you see, if some part of it, something that makes an enzyme maybe – I told you we don't know what we're doing – well, if some of this stuff got loose from the fruit, do you see, and worked its way to the same spot, the reproductive organs, do you see . . .?'

But Joe had sprung to his feet. 'Stop at once. It's too un-dignified. I will not be told I'm a . . . a tree. It's an insult to the sanctity of human nature. It's – why, people are turned to trees in Hell! As a punishment. I know. It's in Dante. I've never read the book because it's much too long, but I've looked at the pictures and there they are, all turned into trees.'

'What for?' asked Harry.

'For doing violence to themselves,' said Joe, still trembling with indignation. 'It was written underneath the picture.'

'He was no fool, Dante,' said Harry, gloomily. 'In a way, that's just what we've been doing.'

There was a long silence between the two men.

'It will wear off,' said Joe. 'Won't it? Harry! Answer me. Say it will wear off.'

'It might. But the effects of one injection on a plant last for three generations.'

'The sins of the fathers,' groaned Joe. 'But I'm *not* a father,' he said, stamping his foot again.

'Not yet,' said Harry, grimly.

'You're quite right. Broods,' said Joe. 'Broods of bastards. I can see them.' He gazed at the sea and the lights of the fishing-boats. 'I know,' he said. 'Got it.'

'What?'

'We shall go straight to a good doctor and tell him everything. There's a wonderful Austrian in Rome who is the soul of discretion and . . .'

'And whose knowledge of biology was twenty-five years out of date when he learned it at his medical school,' said Harry.

'This man's very up-to-date.'

'In reading drug manufacturers' catalogues,' said Harry. 'That's all they have to do nowadays. No, Joe. If you went to a doctor or I did, he'd just gape at us. He might think we were mad. He'd certainly think we were damned comic.'

'Yes,' said Joe. 'That's the really hideous thing about it. You can't say to people, "I'm ill. It's something I've eaten. The symptoms are I have rude dreams and make love to the first woman I see." At least, you could say it, but you wouldn't get much sympathy.'

'That's just the point,' said Harry. 'We're not ill. We're in roaring good health. At least I am. As fit,' he said, bitterly, 'as a fig.'

'Harry, please,' Joe begged. 'None of your coarse phrases. Not tonight.'

*

Half an hour later the whole bay was gleaming with the lights of the fishing-boats, as one by one the late-comers joined their companions. The fishermen rowed in wide circles, laying their nets, and drove the fish before them by thumping on the gunwales of their boats with heavy sticks. The noise of the tattoo, softened by the vast expanse of sea, made the night seem even more silent round the two men on the promontory, like the music of a distant band. They talked in lowered voices, exploring their common misfortune, till at last Joe said:

'So what are we to *do*?'

'We must think of Isabella first,' said Harry.

'Why Isabella? Why not ourselves?'

'Because Isabella thinks you've fallen for her beauty and that I'm half-way to doing the same thing. Whereas the truth is that we'd probably go to bed with a cross-eyed fishwife provided she had the right shape. At least, to judge from my feelings in Salerno in the heat of the day, that's how the stuff works.'

'But we needn't tell Isabella that,' said Joe.

'Perhaps not. But we can't go on making love to her and pinching her behind, knowing what we are. She's a lady.'

'Harry,' said Joe, after a pause, 'you're a snob.'

'Nobody's ever called me that before,' said Harry, in an offended tone.

'Don't get annoyed with me,' Joe answered. 'I rather like snobs. I was a snob myself, just for a while, when I came to Europe. I thought I ought to have another vice besides eating, for the sake of having a balanced personality, if you know what I mean. As far as I could tell from my friends, all the other vices meant sex in one form or another. And I never did go much for that.'

'Nor me, Joe, nor me,' said Harry, emotionally. 'You do believe that, don't you, Joe?'

Joe put his hand on Harry's shoulder.

'Of course I do, Harry. I'm your friend, Harry, and you're mine. We're going to fight this terrible thing side by side.'

'That's right,' said Harry. 'We're pals.'

Joe winced at the word. Then, manfully, he said with solemnity, 'Yes, pals, Harry.'

After a while Harry said, 'I'm sorry. I interrupted you. Why did you give up being a snob?'

'It was the food they gave me when they asked me to their houses. The Dukes and Counts and Baronesses and what not, I mean. They were all in the *Almanach de Gotha* – that's the stud-book, you know – and sometimes I could have sworn they served it up with a brown sauce as an entrée. That's why I took to Isabella. She was so poor that all she could serve me was *spaghetti alla bolognese*, and dam' well cooked it was, too. She's the only one of them that I know, nowadays. I suppose now she thinks I'm in love with her she'll serve dainty suppers for two with a bottle of wine and something in a casserole, like all bachelor women. Quite dreadful.'

Harry suddenly got to his feet.

'Joseph Bellman,' he said firmly. 'Isabella's not going to serve you so much as a lightly boiled egg.'

'What on earth do you mean?'

'She's not going to serve you anything at all, because I'm not going to let you see her. I'm not going to let you see any woman from a distance of under ten feet. And you, Joe are going to do the same thing for me. It's the only way. You put the idea into my head, yourself, when you talked about a balanced personality. Ours is lopsided, isn't it? Well then, we've got to balance it up. We've got to be firm, disciplined, self-controlled, iron-willed. Do you see?'

'Like when you're on a diet,' said Joe, nodding.

'Exactly,' said Harry. 'A moral diet. No women. Like proteins, see. Not the sight or the sound or the smell of 'em. We have the instincts of a particularly depraved billy-goat in the middle of the rutting season . . .'

'Oh, Harry, *please*,' said Joe, and held his breath in terror of what Harry would say next.

'But,' Harry swept on, 'we are still the masters of our fate. We are still the captains of our souls.'

Joe let out his breath in a windy sigh. 'That's much better.' he said. 'And you are so right. We are, aren't we, when you come to think of it.'

'Of course we are,' said Harry. 'It's not often you'll hear me quoting the Bible . . .'

'*Is* that in the Bible?' murmured Joe, doubtfully, but Harry, with a brusque gesture, said:

'Of course it is. I went to Bible class till I was ten and got a gold star for good attendance. As I was saying, I don't often quote the Bible. I'm not a religious man. But I come from a long line of chapel folk, and I am beginning to see now what they were getting at.'

'Oh,' said Joe. 'If you mean I've got to get converted, then I'll have to be a Roman Catholic. All my friends say it's the only one.'

Harry brushed this aside:

'Too soft – too pliable – too much music – too many candles. Besides you can't. Gluttony is one of the seven deadly sins.'

'Not quite,' Joe answered. 'I looked it up. You can eat as much as you like as long as it doesn't take your mind off going to Mass.'

'Quibbles,' said Harry. 'And in any case I'm not asking you to be converted to anything. I mean that just as they used to talk at chapel about wrestling with the Devil, we've got to wrestle with women,' Harry pulled himself up. 'I am a little confused,' he said, 'but I think my point is clear.'

'Quite clear,' said Joe. 'It's just that religion crept in and that confuses even the clearest-headed person, or so I find.

But you're perfectly right when you say we've got to get balanced.'

'And disciplined,' said Harry. 'Mentally disciplined.'

'That reminds me of something. Say it again.'

Harry repeated the phrase, while Joe thought. At last Joe said:

'Got it. It reminds me of my Uncle George.'

'Is that helpful?' asked Harry.

'I don't know,' said Joe, doubtfully. 'Let me think.' Then he, too, jumped to his feet. 'Of course it is,' he said. 'Of course. Harry, do you know Greek?'

'No.'

'Neither do I. Do you know Latin?'

'No.'

'Neither do I. There you are, you see. My Uncle George is one of the trustees who pay me my money every quarter, and whenever I see him he always shakes his head sadly and says, "Joe, if only you'd had the benefit of a classical education." Like him, he means, of course. Uncle George was quite a scholar until the family made up its mind it was time he went into the business. Now he makes things, like the rest.'

'What things?'

'Oom Paul says it's the bit of a guided missile that always goes wrong. Anyway, he's made an enormous amount of money out of it – I mean, replacements and so on, I suppose – and he's always threatening to come out here and retire. "If only," he says to me, "you had the benefits of a classical education, Joe. If only you could understand the gravity of the character of the Romans, the sense of proportion of the Greeks, why, Joe, what a wonderful time you could have in your villa. You can see the severe temples of Paestum from your window" – with binoculars, but George isn't a man for detail, I mean, as the missiles show – well anyway,' Joe tumbled on in his enthusiasm, '"You can see Paestum from your window, and the miracle of Pompeii is round the corner from

62

you. A man who understood what he was seeing might spend the rest of his life there in calm and content." That's what my Uncle George says, and he once sent me a whole pile of books on the subject. I've never opened them. But I'm going to. This very night. And so are you. And tomorrow we're going to set off and see all this balanced calm, the sense of proportion, and in no time at all we'll both be as balanced as a rubber ball on a seal's nose. What do you think, Harry?' Joe finished, out of breath and mopping his brow. He looked at Harry eagerly.

'I say it's a splendid idea,' said Harry. 'It'll keep our minds off women and give us a bit of exercise. I can't go tomorrow. I'll have to get someone to look after the instruments while I'm away. But he can be here by tomorrow evening. Meantime, I have another suggestion. Tonight, we sleep under the same roof.'

'Agreed. You can have the blue guest-room.'

'No,' said Harry, decisively. 'I shall have a bed moved into your room.'

'Well,' said Joe, dubiously. 'I sleep better alone, but ...'

'I'll hear no excuses, Joe. I shall sleep in your room and I shall have a piece of string tied to my big toe. The other end of the piece of string will be tied to your big toe, in case,' said Harry, emphasizing his point with a raised forefinger, 'either you or I, Joe, get it into our heads to go out on the tiles. Agreed?'

'Agreed,' said Joe, fervently, 'pal.'

He held out his hand. Harry took it. They stood in the light of the fishermen's lamp for half a minute with clasped hands, looking gratefully at each other.

Then Joe said, 'Do you know, I'm feeling just a bit – just a little bit – peckish. Let's go down to the house and see what the cook's got for supper.'

*

The string was the only piece of apparatus that Joe would

63

allow to be applied to him. Harry, with his customary methodical ways, had suggested that in the interests of science they should both drive up to the nursing home that stood on the side of one of the mountains of the peninsula, some two thousand feet above them and a mile inland. Joe would have none of it.

'I refuse,' he said, 'to be a guinea-pig; and if you try to make me one, Harry, you will find out why my family calls me "stubborn Joe" – that is, when they're not calling me "daft Joe" or " poor old Joe". I wish guinea-pigs could refuse to be guinea-pigs, too, poor little beasts. I send ten dollars a year to that society which protests against experiments on animals and one hundred dollars to the man who smuggles out news from my family's laboratories about the shocking things that go on in this rocket business. No, Harry. You must just put down in your note-book that *Subject No. 2 never felt better in his life, except for the loss of his appetite.* You can also say he never felt more miserable, if you like.'

But he accepted the string, only insisting that it should be a length of strong silk thread that he had by him. Minu, the butler, moved a bed into Joe's room, and after a light supper they went early to rest.

Minu had spread Harry's bed with the prettiest cover: he had tucked lavender sachets under the pillow, and on the side-table he had daintily arranged a posy of flowers. All this was for Isabella, who, he was sure, would arrive at about midnight when all the servants were supposedly asleep. He was surprised when he saw Harry accompanying Joe into the bedroom and dismayed when he heard the unmistakable sound of Harry taking off his boots. He went down to the kitchen and told them there that he had never thought the master was that sort of man. He said he hoped he wasn't, too, because that sort were usually mean about money. He once more promised Sant' Andrea that he would give up betting on horses.

Meantime, in the bedroom, Harry and Joe prepared themselves for the night.

'Shut your eyes while I tie the knot,' said Harry to Joe, 'then I'll know if you've undone it in the morning. You can do the same for me.'

They then went to bed, each with some books from the classical library. They took, on Harry's advice, a mild sedative. They read for a while, and fell asleep, satisfied, as they told each other when they were drowsing off, that they had done all that two decent men could do.

Joe woke at one in the morning, with a plan, clearly formed in his head, of getting up and going down to the village and throwing a handful of gravel at Isabella's window, which she would open, and seeing him, come down and let him in. The part of the plan which dealt with subsequent happenings was also very clear and most beguiling. He got out of bed, but he had forgotten the string.

Harry woke. He put on the bedside light.

'Is that you, Joe?'

'Yes, Harry.'

'Where are you going, Joe?' asked Harry, sternly.

Joe blushed. He said, in a small voice:

'Please, I want a drink of water.'

'There's water in the jug beside your bed,' said Harry.

'So there is, Harry.'

'Then go back to bed and be good.'

'Yes, Harry,' said Joe, and obeyed.

At three a.m. Harry woke, and again put on the light.

'Joe,' he said. 'Are you awake?'

There was no answer, so he wriggled his big toe. Joe woke.

'Say something, Joe.'

'What?'

'Anything. Anything that comes into your head. But it must be a sentence.'

'"You will be taken from this place and hanged by the neck until you ..."'

'No, no. Not that sort of sentence. I mean one with a subject, object, and verb.'

'Peter Piper picked a peck of pickled peppers. If Peter Piper picked a peck of pickled peppers, where's the peck ...'

'Whoa!' said Harry. 'One's enough. That's a splendid one. Thank you.'

'Can I go to sleep again?'

'Yes,' said Harry, putting out the light. In the darkness Joe heard him muttering, 'Peter; noun, proper subject of sentence, Piper, ditto. Picked, verb, past ... past ... past something.'

'Definite,' supplied Joe. 'What are you doing?'

'Parsing,' said Harry, 'to keep my mind off the Countess's bottom.'

Both men sighed and then, fitfully, but with honour, the long night passed.

*

At breakfast next morning Joe agreed to let Harry go up to the clinic, but insisted that he came with him.

'Nurses,' he said. 'They're women, and quite the worst sort. I mean, for men like us.'

'Quite right,' said Harry. 'Thank you for reminding me. You can drive me up there and I can be back by ten to meet the Director of the microbiological institute from Salerno. I've telephoned him. He says he'll be honoured to help. It'll take about twenty minutes to show him the things he's got to check on, and then we'll be ready for the Greeks.'

The nursing home stood in a forest of chestnut trees. The air was keen and invigorating. Both men felt lighter in spirits. As they drew up at the entrance, Joe even went so far as to wonder if the thing, as they called it between themselves, was wearing off.

'Up here,' he said, 'I feel as pure as a nun.'

The doctor in charge was a Neapolitan who had sunk every penny he owned into the place, and was losing money. He welcomed the two foreigners with tears in his eyes, especially when the matron whispered in his ear the name and size of the long black car they had driven up in. He asked no questions: he barely caught Harry's name: he immediately set about giving him the most elaborate check-up that his apparatus and his fertility of invention could devise.

Joe, having made sure that Harry would not be alone with any of the female staff, except, momentarily perhaps, the matron (who was sixty if a day), left them to their tests.

The tests finished, the doctor cast his eye over his records – or those that were ready on the spot – and noted that Harry was as sound in wind and limb and nerve as the pilot of a supersonic aircraft. He shook his head, and told Harry that if he did not take a complete rest immediately he would not be responsible for him. For the next five minutes he listened while an indignant Harry told him his opinion of the doctor's profession, his degrees, his work, and his dishonesty. Harry also told him who he, Harry Wesley, was. The doctor abjectly promised to send the rest of the tests to Harry's address, and saw him, trembling, to the door.

Harry got into the car. He looked for Joe, but could not see him. The janitor, who was standing by for his tip, said that the gentleman had gone off for a walk in the woods with one of the nurses about fifteen minutes before.

Harry immediately began blowing the horn, in long, persistent blasts that would have set the patients back for weeks in their cure, had there been any. He blew and blew until the doctor, the nurses, and kitchen staff had all come out in alarm on to the front steps.

Finally a short, stout figure came running through the woods.

'Harry!' shouted Joe. 'Thank God, thank God!'

He ran to the car. His hair was dishevelled, his clothing awry. His face was crimson with shame. He scrambled into the driving seat and set the car leaping forward.

'The Greeks,' he cried, 'and the quicker the better.'

ON the drive round the bay to Paestum, Harry gave his friend a severe talking-to. Joe listened humbly. Driving through Salerno, he said (Harry, it would appear, having come to the end of his strictures):

'I agree with everything you say, Harry, and I'm sure I'm sorry it happened. But,' he added, as they drew clear of the city and took the road through the coastal plain, 'there is just one thing you haven't mentioned. It's not only that we behave like goats when we see a woman: the women behave like whores. At least they have on the two occasions that I've made love to them. That nurse, for instance, positively ogled me and when we were in the woods – well, I'm sure I don't know how to undress a nurse in three minutes and it really couldn't have been longer. And Isabella made very little resistance considering her background and her bringing up. It seems they both found me ...' Joe hesitated. 'Look over there, Harry, a bullock cart with Brahmini bulls – they're from India ...'

'They found you what?'

'Irresistible, I think is the word,' said Joe. There was an ominous silence from Harry, and Joe went on in a tiny voice. 'So peaceful, don't you think?'

'What?'

'Bullock carts.'

'I am perfectly certain,' said Harry, 'that Isabella did not find me irresistible. I think that for the sake of the record we might observe that while we have each eaten the same quantity of those damned figs, you have taken two women to bed –'

'Actually, one to bed and one to a fern-clump. For the record,' Joe murmured, apologetically.

'While I,' Harry went on, 'have done no more than pinch one woman on her fully clothed behind.'

'I think you have a firmer character,' said Joe. 'It must be that chapel upbringing. I'm sure it couldn't be anything to do with my being more attractive to women or any nonsense like that.'

'I'm sure it couldn't, too,' said Harry.

'No. Look over there, Harry. A buffalo. That came from India, too. It's part of a government scheme to find animals to suit the climate. It looks very oriental, doesn't it?'

Harry did not answer. After a while, he said :

'That's why there's no need to be *smug* about your two women. The whole thing's purely a chemical reaction.'

'Oh, purely,' agreed Joe. They drove on in silence for a considerable time. Joe stole a look at his companion. He was looking very glum.

'Ah,' said Joe, at length, 'look in the field over there.'

'What is it now?' said Harry, crossly. 'Giraffes?'

'No, Harry. The Greek temples.'

*

The three temples stood in a line, the middle one, built in the purest Doric style, being the biggest and the best preserved. They lay on the coastal plain, facing the hills, with a great stretch of sea and sky behind them. Between them and the sea ran the Sacred Way, bordered with ruins of the ancient city. Beyond that was the town wall, with here and there a tower, still almost intact.

Harry and Joe got out of the car and put some of Uncle George's books in their pockets. They paid their admission at a turnstile and went forward to the temples, more than ever in need of the tranquillizing order and proportion of the Greek things.

'Nothing too much,' said Harry darkly to Joe as they approached the temple. 'That's a Greek motto. I read it last night.'

'I'm sure that wandering among the columns of this beautiful temple will help drive it home to me,' said Joe soothingly. 'What's it called?'

Harry read attentively for a while in one of the books.

'It seems,' he said, 'that the greatest authorities have always ascribed the temple to Neptune, until recently they dug up some votive offerings and found it was the Temple of Hera. Now in science,' Harry went on, looking up from the book, 'we'd call that taking a prat-fall, but I gather that in this branch of knowledge it is called scholarship, and much admired.'

They went up the steps of the Temple of Hera and into the sanctuary. Joe looked about him eagerly. He caught sight of the mountains and then, turning, of the sea between the columns.

'Who but the Greeks,' he exclaimed, 'would have thought of using this particular stone to build with just here? That soft pinkish yellow blends miraculously with the colour of the hills and the colour of the sea. It is a masterpiece of taste, isn't it, Harry?'

Harry, frowning fiercely, was reading some very small print in a footnote.

'Well, the lot that built this temple didn't think so, at any rate,' he said. 'They slapped dead white stucco all over it to make it look like marble. It's all fallen off, but it seems traces of it have been found here and there.'

'White,' said Joe. 'Well, white, too, in its way, you know ... yes, I can see white going very well.'

'You can't have it both ways,' replied Harry. 'If pink and yellow blends with the landscape, then when it was white it must have stuck out like a sore thumb. Well, am I right or aren't I?'

'I think, Harry, you're probably right, but rather muddling, at least for me. I must try hard and concentrate and capture the spirit of the place,' he said, and walked away a few paces among the columns of the portico. Harry unfolded some plans from one of the books and studied them intently.

Meantime, Joe worked conscientiously to let the spirit of Greek things sink into him. He had paid no attention to classical matters. But he had been to school: and he had, for a time, been to Yale. He had listened, if only with half an ear, to a succession of schoolmasters and professors, and from these he had gathered, unconsciously, as we all have, that the Greeks were a people apart. He had been told, as an axiom about which no cultivated man would argue, that there was a rationality, a clarity, a calm, an openness about the Greek mind – a sunlit, clear openness – that laid the foundations of our civilization, whether in science, philosophy, morals, or the arts. This saneness, this clear-eyed humanity, had been inherited (but mishandled) by the Romans and died out of the world with the coming of Christianity, with its gloomy doctrines of an after-life, its obsession with sin, its moral strictures, and its contempt for the humanities. He felt that it was only by some irony of fate that his schoolteachers and professors were living in this Christian – or post-Christian – world. They would have been so much more at home among the Greeks. Some of them, as he knew, felt this so strongly that they spent their whole lives in classical studies, barely troubling about the rest of the world or the remainder of history. Their calm assurance that the Greeks invented all that was worthwhile was thus fortunately undisturbed by the successive discoveries that the Egyptians, the Babylonians, the Persians, the Sumerians, the Indians of the Five Rivers, and the Chaldeans had, in fact, invented nearly all of the things centuries before. Nor did it disturb Joe, who was ignorant all the way down the line from the Greeks to the

Chaldeans. But he knew that it was to the Greeks that a civilized man turned for guidance, and he hoped that they would now still the turmoil in his blood for him, or ease his conscience in a way that would be more agreeable than Harry's chapel-bred strictness. He wanted, he said to himself, to look at this thing philosophically, not morally. He was thoroughly ashamed of what he had been doing. But he could not swear that he had not enjoyed it. It was just the problem for the clean wind of the Greek spirit to blow away.

He thought that he would offer up a prayer to – who was it Harry had said? – ah, yes – to Hera.

'Harry,' he said, walking back, 'where was the altar?'

Harry looked at his plan.

'Outside. It's that mound-like thing by the steps.'

'Is that where they had the statue of the goddess?'

'Oh no. That was inside. The altar was used for cooking.'

'Cooking?' said Joe, his interest suddenly roused beyond his hopes.

'Yes. On high days and holidays and bonfire nights, as we used to say as kids, the Greeks used to drag oxen and goats and baskets of pigeons and God knows what, slit their throats, and throw them on to a wood fire on the altar. When they were done to a turn they were eaten.'

'How utterly barbarous, Harry!'

'Yes. The poor beasts must have smelt the blood and gone frantic. I was reading last night one of them got away and had to be pole-axed. Everybody was very fed up because it . was considered a bad omen. The noise, the stink, the blood, and the clamour! They used to blow on pipes and beat tambourines. Just think of it. It must have been like a revivalist meeting being held in a fully functioning slaughter yard.'

'Well, yes, that, of course. But how could the Greeks of all people have eaten meat that was merely flung on a fire?' said Joe, with a shudder. 'It couldn't have been much better than a barbecue, and barbecues were one of the reasons, I may tell you, that I am glad my family persuaded me to live outside the United States.'

Joe looked at the remains of the altar for a while with an expression of alarm and disgust. Then he said:

'But don't tell me, Harry, that those beautiful white statues of gods and goddesses that I've seen in museums were bloodstained.'

'No,' Harry answered. 'They weren't. They were kept inside. Just about there,' he said, and pointed to a spot some two-thirds of the way down the middle of the interior of the temple. Joe walked back and stood silently on the place that Harry had indicated. The sanctuary – for that was where he was standing – was closed in by columns smaller than those on the exterior, and there were two rows of them, one row standing on the architrave of the row beneath. Even though the temple had lost its roof, there was a feeling of intimacy, of quiet, and of decorum. Joe stood, thinking, for several minutes. Then Harry, the plans flapping out of his book, his forefinger thrust between the pages marking a place, walked down the temple and joined him. He saw that Joe was looking upwards at a spot about fifteen feet above him. He followed Joe's gaze.

'See anything interesting, Joe?'

'Yes, Harry. The statue of the goddess Hera.'

'That you can't,' said Harry, 'because it's gone. Vanished. Nothing left. They didn't even find the tip of her nose.'

'I can see it,' said Joe, patiently, 'in my imagination.'

'Good for you, Joe.'

'Tall, white, graceful. The figure of a benign woman. A beautiful, benign, *chaste* woman. I can see her looking down at me.'

'Can you?' said Harry. 'Well, she's got painted blue eyes. Check? Painted lips, gilt hair, rouged cheeks like a doll's, and dangling ear-rings. Check? That's what it says in the book that the statues looked like. They don't say what colour the frock was, but it was probably red with purple stripes. It seems the Greeks were great ones for a splash of colour once they got a paint brush in their hands. Oh, yes, and this painted trollop stood on a boat. But, of course, with your imagination, you don't need me to tell you that, do you?'

'A boat?' said Joe. 'How bizarre. No, my imagination hadn't run to a boat.'

'It says here . . .' said Harry, pointing to his book, but Joe held up his hand.

'If it says there that they impaled unwanted babies on the prow or some similar horror, I don't want to hear it. You're spoiling my mood, Harry.'

'Just giving you the facts, old boy.'

'I think one can have too many facts in a place like this.'

Harry grinned. 'I bet that's what the man who called it the Temple of Neptune thought, when they dug up the bit of pottery which said it wasn't.'

'Maybe. But there's something I want to say.'

'Shoot.'

'It's about that nurse and Isabella.'

Harry frowned. 'We're here to forget them,' he said.

'That's just it,' said Joe, with enthusiasm. 'In a way, I have.'

'A damned funny way,' said Harry. 'Dragging them by their back hair into the middle of a ruin.'

'It's not that I want to talk about them, Harry. It's just that – well, here, I can.'

Harry sighed theatrically. 'Well, since there's no stopping you, let's have it. We got as far as the fern-clump. Take it from there.' He sat down with heavy resignation on a fallen block.

'You misunderstand me,' said Joe. 'What I want to say is – look; you remember how miserable and ashamed I was when I came out of the woods: as miserable and ashamed as I was after I – well, after Isabella?'

'So you ought to be,' said Harry, truculently.

'Yes, but that's your chapel upbringing,' Joe explained. 'I agree with you. I wasn't brought up chapel, but after all, we're all Christians, nowadays, even those of us like you and me who wouldn't dream of going to church. We've got a Christian sense of sin.'

'If what you are wanting to tell me is that it is unchristian to fling yourself slavering with lust on to two innocent women, I think,' said Harry, firmly, 'that you're probably correct, although I would not claim to be a theological expert. It's not only unchristian, it's a lot of other things besides and . . .'

'Wait, Harry. What I mean is, supposing, on the other hand, I was a Greek. Suppose I had made love to two women . . .'

'The way you keep saying that over and over again makes me think of charades,' said Harry. 'I'm sure it's a clue to the proverb we've got to guess.'

'If I were a Greek, in the old days,' Joe persisted, 'I'd come here to this temple, all washed and perfumed, in a clean white garment, with a wreath of roses on my head.'

'Roses?' said Harry, and laughed.

'Well, maybe I haven't got the facts right. What would I be wearing, then?'

'Roses suit me fine,' said Harry and laughed again. 'Go on.'

'Then I'd raise my hands to the goddess, like this,' said Joe, copying a gesture he remembered seeing on a Greek vase, 'and I'd offer a prayer to her. "Goddess," I would say, "I have just made. . ."'

'. . . love to two women,' Harry supplied. 'One in bed and one in a fern-clump. What would you say then?'

Joe let down his hands. 'I'd say, "Thank you, Hera. I rather enjoyed it,"' he said, with great simplicity.

Harry was silent.

'You see, Harry, I wouldn't have a sense of sin. The goddess wouldn't be looking down at me and saying, "What have you been doing and don't do it again." I remember how Uncle George used to tell me that the Greek religion was a pure, joyous worship of the powers of the universe. It wasn't going in front of a magistrate, as the Christians made it. Uncle George used to say that the Greek religion was just a beautiful theory about what made the universe tick. It had something open, fresh, and childlike about it. Standing here, I do feel Uncle George was right.'

'Ho, *yes?*' said Harry. 'Ho, *yes*? Then let me tell you your Uncle George never read the books he fobbed off on you.' He searched rapidly in one of the volumes he was carrying and unfolded a long chart, covered with what appeared to be a genealogical tree. 'You want to know how things really got going? Eh? Well, just look here,' he said, pointing to the chart. 'It seems that Uranus – that was the god of the sky – had his balls cut off. They were cut off by one of his sons, whom he had previously eaten. Don't ask me to explain that, ask your Uncle George. Anyhow, here was this Uranus with his balls cut off, and they were thrown into the sea. I don't know how the sea was created, and I'd rather not be pressed on the question. The answer might not be nice. Well, from these balls Aphrodite was born, and by a series of matings and love-affairs that would make a chicken farmer shade his eyes in shame, so were all this mob of gods, goddesses, and heaven knows what that you see here in the small print. Now as a theory about the evolution of the universe, I admit that I've heard damned-sight sillier ones put up by renowned physicists. But you can tell your Uncle George that if a child of nine came along to me with that story, I'd have the hide off him. And talking of what makes things tick,' he said, stubbing his finger at another part of the chart, 'look down here. You've heard of Nemesis, haven't you? It was the Greek equivalent of Einstein's formula of energy and mass.

Do you know what happened to Nemesis? Zeus chased her to the end of the earth, where she turned into a goose and he turned into a swan and they mated. Probably in a fern-clump. Changing into animals seemed a popular form of making love. Look at this bit here. Poseidon – he was the god of the sea – fell in love with Demeter – she was the goddess of the earth. So they pop into bed together. Just before they turned out the light, she turned into a mare and he turned into a horse. Why? Just to make it more interesting, I suppose. And what happened from that little get-together? Well, what do you think *would* happen. She gave birth to one daughter, and one horse. It seems that the Old Man of the Sea was rather disappointed by this outcome, or so it says here, because he married again. This time he picked on Amphitrite. Probably learning from experience, he didn't change into anything, and neither did she. They had six sons. But it didn't turn out any better. All six of the sons raped their mother. So Poseidon drowned the lot of them – shocked, I suppose, to learn of such goings-on in his family. Meantime, Joe, our little Aphrodite – remember her? – hadn't been letting the grass grow under her feet. She got herself married to Hermes, and produced a nice little family. One of them was Priapus, and the other was Hermaphroditus. I gather from this chart that the names, so to speak, suggested themselves to the children's doting mother. I could go on but I won't, because I know you have an aversion to listening to too many facts. But all I can say is that if your Uncle George considers all that pure, fresh, and childlike, then he must be quite a card when it comes to telling a smoking-room story.'

*

Nobody likes to hear a close relative called a fool, even if he privately believes his relative to be a jackass. Joe summoned all his abilities to defend his Uncle George, if not from conviction, then from a sense of honour. A thought came to him

– an increasingly frequent thing with him since he had met Harry. He mustered his best Yale manner. He even drew in his stomach.

'I should like,' he said, 'to hear all that again.' He paused. 'In Greek,' he said.

'Why?'

'Because, my dear Harry, there's no denying you have a very vivid way of putting things. But your vocabulary – oh, I admire it: I suppose you must have learned it after Sunday school was over – your vocabulary, my friend, is Anglo-Saxon. Now my Uncle George once told me that the Greeks spoke the most perfect language ever devised by the mind of man. It was wonderfully supple and expressive and nobody has ever succeeded in writing verses which sounded so grand and so beautiful. My Uncle George quoted some verses, from Homer I think it was, to prove his point. Now it seems to me that if Homer had told the stories that you have just told me the effect – forgive me, Harry, comparisons are odious, I know – but it seems to me that the effect would have been more – ah – cultivated.'

He pulled up his trousers and sat down on a block of stone. He put his hands on his knees. He looked at Harry, smiling. He felt he had done rather well. Harry's expression was blank. Then Harry drew a long breath. A light came into his eyes.

'Did *you* think it was beautiful?' he said, in a humbly inquiring tone. 'The poetry that your uncle quoted, I mean.' Joe was delighted to see that his little thrust had brought down some of Harry's bumptiousness.

'Confidentially, Harry, when Uncle George quoted Greek, as he did very frequently before they gave him the job of making the thing that goes wrong in missiles, it always seemed to me that he was saying over and over again ... wait a minute ... I must remember the line I made up ... ah, yes.' He deepened his voice, ' "Oh," he said, "*behold! That coxcomb's gone and hoist a block of gingham.*" That was the sort of sound it made.'

Harry laughed.

'But I've got no ear for poetry. I've no doubt that to a sensitive listener the thing sounds sublime.'

'I should have liked to have heard your Uncle George recite,' said Harry. 'Just for five minutes.'

'Oh yes,' said Joe, affably. 'I wish you could. I mean when I spoke of sensitive listeners, I wasn't excluding you. Oh, dear me, no.'

'Because,' said Harry, ignoring him, 'at the end of that five minutes I would like to read your Uncle George a passage from this admirable compendium of useful knowledge,' he said, tapping an open page of the book in his hand, 'which is called a *Compendium of Greek Studies*. It says, I quote, "The one certain thing about the pronunciation of the Greek language is that our own way of speaking it is purely arbitrary. We may be quite sure that if we quoted one line of poetry to a classical Greek, he would find our accent totally incomprehensible, and, in all likelihood, risible." Risible,' said Harry, closing the book, 'is a very nice word. Scholarly, I call it. Like your uncle.'

'Harry,' said Joe, rising, 'that settles it. There is a limit to one's duty to one's family. For all I care you can chase that charlatan of an uncle of mine three times round this temple and pole-axe him on the high altar to the sound of flutes. I quite see that that classical gentleman has been having me on a string.'

'Like all the rest of the classical gentlemen, if you ask me,' said Harry. 'Not that I blame them. If every time someone tells you he's cleverer, brainier, and better educated than you are, you just open your mouth and nod your head, he's bound to take advantage of you. Look at us – the scientists, I mean. You put us on a pedestal, bang your foreheads on the ground and say, "Speak, O Mage!" And we speak. We speak with the volubility of a charwoman invited to describe the twinges she gets in her joints. Among the things I remember scientists saying is that if anybody split the atom the world would blow up in a chain reaction. Very convincing it was. Then there was the man who said he'd worked it out that we'd all starve to death by A.D. 2050. Gave me quite a turn, he did, when I was a boy. He quite altered my life. Just for the sake of curiosity, I went over his arithmetic a little while ago. He'd got his sums wrong. I don't suppose he even tried to get them right. And it seems to me this classical racket's just about the same. Chaps like your Uncle George and all the rest read a few books that they like and then say what's expected of them for the rest of their lives. The rest of us say, "How scholarly", and give your Uncle George honorary degrees for saving us the trouble of using our brains.'

'He was just about to get one when the family made him the general manager of the missile plant,' said Joe.

'Whereas,' went on Harry, 'if they told the truth, they would tell us what sticks out a mile to anybody who takes the trouble to open an honest book, that the Greeks were fluent liars with dirty minds.'

'Oh, come, come,' said Joe, protestingly.

'And that,' said Harry, 'I did not learn behind the chapel after Sunday school, but inside it during the service. Old Reverend Peebles said it in a sermon. Real down on the Greeks, he was, and he could read their language, too. I've never forgotten what he said, and it looks as though he was right.' Harry picked up the chart of the gods and scanned it, shaking his head.

Joe said:

"Yes, but wasn't it one of the great virtues of the Greeks that they called a myth a myth and not a dogma? At least I seem to have heard it said. I mean your Reverend Peebles probably believed every word of his religion. But I don't think the Greeks believed in their religion at all.'

'No?' said Harry. 'Well, what about this? Let me see,' he said, putting down one book and taking up another. It was in the chapter on Sicily. I remember reading it up in the car because I thought we might do a trip . . . ah!' he exclaimed. 'Got it. It's a footnote.' He read it attentively, mumbling a little. 'Yes. It seems the Athenians had a war on with Syracuse. They sent two of their best generals across the water to fight it. But the day after they left, the Athenians discovered that some clown had gone round in the night mutilating some statues of the gods. I suppose that's scholarly for knocking off their packets. Anyway, these intelligent, balanced, sceptical Athenians who knew a myth when they saw one, yelled, "Blasphemy!" as one man. Like a meeting of the Sunday Observance Society it must have been. Then they decided that it was Alcibiades who had done it. So what do you think they did? They sent a fast ship to arrest this general on the high seas and bring him back for trial. The only person who seems to have behaved with a grain of commonsense in the matter was this same Alcibiades. He went absent-without-leave and joined up with the enemy. That left Nicias to fight the war. He gave battle just outside Syracuse but lost it. Why? Because between the two armies was a temple to a god to whom this egregious pillar of the Church was particularly partial. He wouldn't let his soldiers harm it. He not only lost the battle, he lost the war and his army, who were sent to the quarries. He was subsequently very proud of the way he conducted the campaign, particularly the temple bit.'

'Generals are always proud of their most disastrous mistakes,' said Joe. 'I noticed that when I read military history at Yale. Unfortunately I wrote it in an examination paper and that, I think, is why I was given gamma minus.'

'That's just a red herring,' said Harry, severely. 'You don't want to admit that you're wrong. But you are. Reverend Peebles, the Old Bull of Bashan, from what I can recall of him, would certainly be willing to lose a battle for a church parade. But nobody would let him. Then there's Alcibiades. What have you to say to that?'

'Nothing,' said Joe. 'You've made your point with me there.'

'Good,' said Harry. 'I'll give you Plato and Socrates and all that crowd,' he said expansively, showing that he could be generous in victory. But Joe said:

'You don't have to, Harry. As a matter of fact, I know something about them already. One day when I was looking through Uncle George's books to see if there was just one that I could bring myself to read – George was coming over to stay a month, I remember, but he never made it – I came across a book called *Plato's Symposium*, or *The Banquet*. The subtitle naturally attracted me, so I put it beside my bed. I thought it might be interesting to know what the Greeks ate. Well, I read it from time to time. I hadn't got more than a quarter of the way through when I felt in my bones that something was very wrong. I know a good deal about banquets, and one thing I was sure of, Greeks or not, nobody ever talked as these characters talked over a table. So I turned to the introduction to find out something more about the book. Well, I was right. The thing wasn't meant to be real. It was a literary confection of Plato's. One of the principal characters was Socrates – another, by the way, was your friend Alcibiades – and the piece purported to be a record of his remarks. Now being a victim of what you call the classical racket, I had always thought that Socrates was one of the world's greatest men. Mind you, I knew nothing whatever about him ...'

'Aha!' said Harry.

'And to my surprise,' went on Joe, 'I found there was practically nothing to know. Scholars, if you'll forgive the word, have been working for years to establish one thing that Socrates must have said himself, as distinct from something a writer put in his mouth. Do you know what they discovered?'

'No.'

'Sweet,' said Joe, savouring the words, 'Fanny Adams.'

Harry chuckled.

'He might have said the things they wrote, but it's much more likely, so I understand, that it is all a beautiful legend – or lie as you would say – got up for the purposes of political propaganda. Plato and his set were what we would call authoritarians in their views. But the rest of the Athenians weren't. So there you are. You have committed mayhem on their religion, I have disposed of Socrates, so all we've got left to say in praise of them is that they were fine artists.'

'Oh, *artists*,' said Harry, with profound contempt.

'There speaks the authentic voice of the Reverend Peebles,' said Joe. 'Come, let's walk a bit. These stones are getting hot now the sun is on them.'

They came down the Sacred Way and came to some ruins that once had been the forum. There was a great confusion of chambers, corridors, and blind alleys, built in the days when the Greeks had gone and Paestum had become a Roman city.

Harry went from chamber to chamber, examining the walls.

'What are you looking for?' Joe asked.

'Dirty pictures.'

'I didn't know the Greeks went in for that sort of thing.'

'Maybe they didn't. But this forum is Roman. It reminds me of Pompeii. And Pompeii is as full of them as a brothel.'

'What a wide range of experience you have,' said Joe, with gentle malice. 'Now *I* have never been inside a brothel.'

'Neither have I,' said Harry. 'That's just it. I used to be rather ashamed of the fact. I thought I was a prig. Well, maybe I am a prig at that. But that's my whole point. Or perhaps to be fair, I think it's probably the Reverend Peebles's point. You see, with these Greeks and Romans it was sex, sex,

sex, morning, noon, and night. Sex in religion, sex on the living-room wall, sex in the theatre . . .'

'Sex at mealtimes,' added Joe. '*The Banquet* is almost entirely about a reprehensible affair between two men. Lord Chesterfield . . .'

'Yes, you told me,' said Harry. 'Well, as I see it, that couldn't have been all the fun that everybody desperately made it out to be.'

'Oh, I don't know . . .'

'Forget the fern-clump for a moment, if you can,' said Harry. 'This wasn't a scrimmage in the woods. It went *on*. It was organized. There were whole professions looking after it. It was something you had to do to be thought well of like . . . like . . .'

'Watching baseball,' said Joe. 'But you wouldn't know what I mean, fortunately. Still, they must have got *some* fun out of it.'

'Cooks spend their lives cooking food, and tasting it all day long. Do they like it, as you like it?'

'I'm damned if they do,' said Joe. 'I've never had a cook with a sensitive palate yet. They taste for the salt, or the cinnamon. Never for the whole sauce.'

'Exactly. So my point is this. When those early Christians came along and said, "All this sex isn't fun and it isn't doggy and it isn't smart. It's Original Sin" – well, it was a push-over. As soon as there were enough of them to make a tolerably sized organization, they walked off with Greece and Rome and the Empire and the Emperor included. The prigs were right. The prigs were just what everyone was waiting for.'

Joe thought for a little.

'It's certainly ironic,' he said, 'that a man who holds the views you do – and I don't dispute them, Harry – should go down in history as the discoverer of . . . well . . . Wesley's figs.'

'The Copernicus of the bedroom,' he said. 'Ah well, let's hope the whole thing will wear off. I can't say this trip's got our minds off sex, but I feel it's strengthened our moral attitude towards the problem. Don't you?'

Joe did not answer. He was looking past Harry. He had a most curious expression on his face.

'Harry,' he said, 'unless your figs are capable of producing a mirage in broad daylight, there is a woman some forty yards behind you, who is taking off all her clothes.'

*

She had undressed as far as her chemise, and she was shaking out her yellow hair. She was in an alcove of Roman brickwork, part of some place of public resort on the far confines of the ancient town. The alcove, which was one of many, faced the prospect of the shore and sea. It had been built, perhaps, as a place to go to catch the rare summer breezes.

She pulled her chemise over her head and threw it on a stone. She revealed herself as a handsomely built young woman, deep-breasted, long-legged, and in spite of being brown from the Italian sun, here and there it could be seen that she had a fair white skin. She was dressed now solely in two exiguous coverings, and even these she rolled into a still smaller compass. She then stretched her arms above her head, and, shortly afterwards, lay down on what remained of the marble paving. But since a low wall divided the alcoves from the adjacent ruins, she disappeared from Joe and Harry's view.

'It's an outrage,' said Harry, indignantly. 'This isn't a bathing-beach. It is a venerable monument of antiquity. It belongs to the whole civilized world and that girl is using it as though she's hired it for half a crown. I wouldn't be surprised if she didn't put up a beach umbrella.'

Instead of an umbrella, she raised one shapely bare leg in the air so that it was visible above the parapet, and then followed it with the other. She then circled her legs and semaphored with them for a while.

'Hip-reducing exercises,' said Harry. 'Here, in the middle of Paestum!'

'Well,' said Joe, 'on the perimeter really. I didn't know you thought so highly of the place.'

'My criticisms of it were an objective search for the truth. This,' said Harry, climbing on a fallen column so that he could see over the parapet, 'is vandalism. She looks German. I'm sure she is. They burned the ships at Nemi, remember? I think we should protest.'

'Can you see better from up there?'

'I *could*,' said Harry, stepping down quickly, 'but I have seen quite enough. I am going straight to one of the custodians to lay a complaint. No. Better. You go and lay a complaint. Your Italian is more colloquial than mine. I shall stay here and watch what she gets up to next. Bring the custodian straight back so he can see with his own eyes.'

'Well,' said Joe, 'I'm not much of a one for making protests, but I must say I do hate damned tourists – the beach maniacs, I mean – and I don't mind having a slap at them. I found three of them having a picnic underneath my own terrace last year, and they were quite huffy when I turned them out. Yes, Harry,' he decided, as the legs went once again into the air and described circles, 'I think you're right. I'll get the man to come over and stop her.'

He trotted back along the Sacred Way on his short legs, crossly remembering the picnic party, the people in a rowboat who had played a radio under his window all night, and a dozen other vexations of living on the shores of the sea to which visitors from all Europe come like lemmings each summer, but unfortunately (according to Joe) do not, like lemmings, drown in it.

He made his way past the Temple of Hera, and went to the wooden building that stood to one side of the entrance turnstile. He found a man in uniform, who alternately pulled on a cigarette and yawned prodigiously. He was grey-haired, and his long-nosed face had that expression of settled and sour gloom that is so often the mark of the Neapolitan.

'Guard,' said Joe, 'I am sorry to inform you that there is a woman – a foreigner by all appearances – who has taken off her clothes and is sunbathing in the northwest sector of the ruins.'

The guard looked Joe up and down slowly. He studied Joe's shoes. He priced them. It is again characteristic of the Neapolitan that he believes he can find out everything he needs to know about a stranger from what he puts on his feet. Joe's shoes were shabby, as they always were, because Joe did not like to draw attention to his feet, which he thought absurdly small and dainty for a man of his corpulence. The custodian decided that Joe was lower-middle class.

'Sunbathing?' he said, looking up. 'Yes, I know. She likes it.' He paused. 'I like it, too,' he said. 'Something for me to look at besides rows of bloody columns.'

'But this is a celebrated place,' said Joe. 'People come all across the world to study it – scholars, professors, experts. They don't want a semi-nude woman cluttering up the landscape.'

'Why not?' asked the custodian. 'I'd say she was a sight for their sore eyes. Besides, I bet she knows more about these ruins than any one of them. She's been here every day for a month. Swede, she is. She says she lived here two thousand years ago. It came to her one night, looking at the midnight sun or something. Nice girl, she is, too. Wishes me a civil good day, coming and going, and offers me a cigarette. No trouble at all. Not like some foreigners who buy a ticket and then think they own the place. One of them will be wanting me to shift the columns round a bit to meet his taste better, I shouldn't wonder.' The custodian stared at Joe with his mournful eyes.

'My friend over there,' said Joe, a little weakly, 'wants to make a protest. In the name of civilized people everywhere,' he added, with a little attempt at a bluster, which made no impression at all on the melancholy custodian.

'There's no reason why he shouldn't,' said the custodian. 'He should write a letter to the Superintendent of Antiquities of the province of Salerno.'

'Will he do something about it?'

'Certainly he will. Since the lady in question is a Swede and a Swede is a foreigner he will send the letter on to the Bureau of Strangers of the Prefecture for suitable action. When they look up her files they will find she isn't a resident but a temporary visitor, so they will send the letter up to Rome to the Department of Tourism for handling.'

'Well, they ought to take action,' said Joe. 'They ought to take action in a lot of instances in my opinion.'

'They'll take action all right,' said the custodian, still without any change from his melancholy expression. 'They'll see that the incident took place in a scheduled monument so they'll send it to the Department of Fine Arts. Don't ask me where it'll go after that because I've never followed one further. Anyway, it'll be about November then, and November's pretty chilly round these parts, so I daresay she'll have packed and gone. More's the pity, I say. I like her. And so,' he said, a trace of a smile appearing for the first time on his gloomy face, 'does your friend, by the looks of it.'

He pointed. Joe turned. In the north-eastern corner of the ruins he saw the girl, now dressed in some sort of wrap, walking slowly along the end of the Sacred Way. Harry was walking beside her and his arm was tightly round her waist.

Someone rattled with a coin on the turnstile.

'Customers,' said the custodian. 'I must be going.'

Joe mumbled something in reply and then set off at a run towards Harry and the girl. But the Sacred Way was long and Joe's legs were short. By the time he had come to the end of the way they had disappeared.

Joe searched frantically for them, stumbling into ruined houses, tripping over marble blocks, and ducking into brick tunnels. But they were not to be seen. He found a gateway in the wall and a set of broken steps and stood on top of the wall. He looked round him. He could see the whole range of the ruins, the beach, and the sea. A large party of visitors was just making its way to the Temple of Hera. The beach, it seemed, was deserted.

Then Joe saw Harry and the girl lying underneath some juniper bushes that grew in the sand-dunes near the wall. They were in a close embrace. It was too late, Joe reflected, for even a pal to do anything to save Harry. He climbed down from the rampart.

For the next half-hour he patrolled the Sacred Way, on guard to warn his friend if the party of visitors should be approaching his trysting place.

*

The visitors went round the principal temple, and left, shepherded by a restless guide who kept looking at his watch. Once more the ruins were deserted. Joe walked for a while among them wondering what he should do for the best. He recalled that Harry, in a similar situation, had sounded the horn of the car. But it was too far away and there was no road to bring it nearer. He thought of going back to his vantage point on the wall and throwing, perhaps, warning stones.

Harry would be grateful. But then there was the Swede. It was clear that she was a woman with a mind of her own. Would she resent being stoned in the middle of an embrace? Would she perhaps stone him back? He settled, at last, for going to the gateway in the wall and calling out to the sand-dunes, 'Harry! It's time we were going!' He looked fixedly in the direction opposite to that in which he knew Harry was to be found, and he called three times. He felt he had done his duty. He went back to the Sacred Way to wait.

Ten minutes passed, and Harry did not come. Twenty minutes passed, and forty. The sun shone down fiercely on the ruins and Joe sought the shade of a wall. He sat down. He caught himself dozing. He got up and decided to go to the entrance turnstiles where he remembered that there was a small room with a counter for selling postcards, and some chairs. It would be cooler and more comfortable to wait there.

When he got to the turnstiles the Neapolitan custodian came out of his ticket office to meet him.

'Ah, there you are,' he said. 'I was just coming to look for you. Your moralistic friend has left a message for you. He isn't feeling well and he's waiting at the bar across the road. He looked for you, but couldn't find you.'

'Thank you,' said Joe. 'I'll go over to him straight away.'

'Looks pretty cut up,' said the custodian. 'I reckon she gave him a slap round the chops.'

'No,' said Joe, sadly. 'I'm rather afraid she didn't. Here's something for your trouble.' He left the man muttering his thanks. He walked down the road. He saw Harry sitting, woebegone, at a table outside a small café. Harry was staring at the ground; his hands were hanging limply between his legs. His hair was in disorder and an empty cognac glass was beside him.

Joe looked at him with compassion. 'I must be very gentle with him,' he said to himself. 'After all, poor Harry, in a way, has suffered a fate worse than death.'

He crossed the road and joined his friend.

*

It was on the way back to Salerno that Harry came to his decision. On the right hand of the road lay a great arc of hills, and between them, cool and blue in the distance, were the peaks of the spine of the Apennines. Harry watched them for a while. Then he said:

'Joe. Stop the car. I've made up my mind.'

Joe put on the brakes.

'I'm going for a hike,' said Harry.

'A *hike*?' said Joe. 'That's quite the most hideous of all your ugly words, Harry. Do you mean you want to get out and walk a little? By all means. I'll follow slowly in the car.'

'Not where I'm going,' said Harry. He pointed to the hills. 'I'm going to get as far away from the roads as I can.'

'But Harry,' Joe protested, 'you can't go for a ... a ... walking tour in the Apennines. It's unthinkable. They're much too wild and lonely.'

'The wilder and lonelier the better. I've got to get fresh air into my lungs, Joe, fresh mountain air. Maybe it'll blow this awful thing away. Come with me,' said Harry, but without any great enthusiasm.

'I've never walked two miles in my life,' said Joe. 'I'd only be a nuisance. Well, if you've made up your mind, let's go and have lunch and buy some things and ...'

'I don't need to buy anything and I'll get some lunch at the first village I pass. I'm setting off now, Joe. Right away. It's the only thing to do. I'm sorry you're not coming with me. But to tell you the truth, it was going to be pretty shaming, driving home with you, after all the things I said to you on the way here. No, Joe. I'll go off and I'll be back home tomorrow. I've hiked before when I was in trouble.'

'Is there anything I can do for you?' Joe asked, anxiously. 'How are you off for money?'

'Plenty,' said Harry, producing his wallet.

'Have you got your passport?'

'No.'

'But, my dear fellow, you can't go wandering about Italy without your passport. They won't let you in hotels.'

'Then I'll sleep out or knock on someone's door.'

'But if something happens, Harry. Have you got anything to identify you?'

'Will this do? It's a letter from Pozzo.'

'I suppose it will have to,' said Joe. 'But . . .'

'There's one thing you can do for me. Tell the Director to stay on at my house. He'll be delighted. He thinks I'm the biggest thing that's happened in his provincial little life. Oh yes – and lend me a map.'

They said good-bye. Harry strode off down a path that led straight into the heart of the hills. Joe drove homewards.

When Joe arrived at the village near which he lived, he felt tired and hungry and lonely.

He saw Isabella sitting in her garden and he stopped the car, thinking to say a few words and then to drive on. She was delighted to see him. She saw that he was tired. She divined that he was lonely, and he admitted that he wanted something to eat. She cooked him an omelette. They ate it together. She gave him some coffee. They drank it together. Then they went to bed and made love.

At that very moment Harry was sitting on a hilltop. He was munching bread and olives and from time to time he took a swig from a bottle of country wine.

He drew in a great breath of mountain air and slowly, luxuriously exhaled it. He put back his shoulders.

'It's passing off,' he said aloud. 'I swear the filthy thing is passing off. And to think that my old head master was right all the time. All I needed was some vigorous exercise.'

*

Joe lay in bed beside Isabella, tackling a moral problem. The afternoon sun crept into the room between the bars of the green shutters on the window that looked out to sea. The window that opened on to the garden had its shutters folded back and Joe could see an oleander tree covered in its first blooms. The room was filled with the sleepy quiet of a

Mediterranean afternoon. It was a good environment for tackling a moral problem – peaceful, relaxed, undemanding – if only one could remember for ten consecutive minutes what the problem was.

Isabella stirred on her pillow. Joe's mind wandered luxuriously. He reflected that if only he had known that there were women who did not automatically light cigarettes after making love, he might have been to bed with more of them. He saw with approval that there was not even an ashtray in Isabella's room. She would make as good a wife as she made a housekeeper.

Joe stared at the strips of sunlight in the ceiling. 'Ah, yes,' he said to himself, 'a wife. That, of course, was the problem.'

A little later he said:

'Isabella.'

'Yes, Joe.'

'I'm thinking ...' He paused.

'Yes, Joe. What about?'

'Well, about love and that sort of thing.'

'Oh, Joe. Not *afterwards*!'

'But what else should I be thinking about?' said Joe, bewildered.

'Well, as for me,' said Isabella, 'I think about the household accounts, and gardening, and the letters that I ought to have answered. I couldn't say what men think about: whether it's time to buy a new car, perhaps.' Seeing Joe frown, she went on, 'I mean, Joe, one thinks about making love for hours and days and even months before it happens. And when it does happen, the most lovely thing about it is that you do not have to think about making love any more – at least, for a time.'

'But surely,' said Joe, 'if a man makes love and then immediately starts thinking of buying a new auto, he's behaving exactly like an animal.'

'I wonder,' said Isabella, dreamily, 'what sort of animal

would think about buying an auto after making love? I know: a French poodle. One of those white ones, with jewelled collars, that seem to live in cars all their lives. Or perhaps you can think of a better one?'

'I'm thinking of something quite different,' said Joe. He was thinking, in fact, that every decent instinct in him told him that he should confess to Isabella just what had happened to him. On the other hand, he had given his word to Harry that he would not tell anybody at all. That was the moral issue. He shut his eyes against the sunlight and the oleanders and did his best to deal with it.

After some considerable thought, he opened his eyes again and looked at Isabella lying calmly and reposefully beside him.

'Put it this way,' said Joe. 'When a man and a woman make love – I mean while they are actually in each other's arms – they think about each other, don't they?'

'No,' said Isabella, punching up the cushions so that she could lean against them. 'They think about themselves.'

'You mean he thinks about himself and she thinks about herself?'

'Of course. How else could a husband and wife who've been married for years still make love together? If they thought about each other, they'd be fighting within five minutes.'

'Yes, I suppose that's true,' said Joe, thoughtfully. 'Go on talking, Isabella. Do, please. I've such a lot to learn. What with being thought a fool and having an excellent butler, now that I'm middle-aged, I've led a sheltered life.'

'Well,' said Isabella, 'everybody talks about making love as though it's a ... a *chummy* thing,' she said, remembering a word from her English sojourn. 'But it isn't, really. It's ... the thing itself ... just *that*, I mean ... is about as personal as waving to a passing train. There's a general feeling of *bonhomie* to nobody in particular. What matters is getting what you want, preferably on your own terms. Women – and always remember that women are silly chits, Joe – are always dreaming of love from a stranger. The fact is that if they weren't so vain they'd realize they never get it from anybody else.'

'Then I needn't have worried,' said Joe, half to himself.

'No,' said Isabella, 'you needn't worry at all.'

'All the same, when a man asks a woman to marry him, surely he means, "My darling, let us get married because you are the only woman in the whole wide world that I shall ever want to go to bed with?"'

'He does,' said Isabella. 'Then he needs a church, an organ, a ring, a sermon, a breakfast, and about a hundred people in their best clothes to drive into his silly head what a thundering lie he's got to live up to. And if he dodges these, there's the law about alimony to do the same thing for him.'

'But why did he tell it in the first place?' Joe asked.

'I think he says it because he hopes it will be true,' said Isabella. 'He hopes he will only need one woman all his life. It will leave him more time for running his business, or practising his golf, or catching up with his reading. Joe, you know you're rather an exception. Most men haven't got the passionate nature you've got. They like to think they have. But I've come to the conclusion that their favourite piece of furniture isn't the bed; it's an arm-chair.'

'You think I'm different?'

'You are.'

This so disturbed Joe that he got out of bed and began dressing. He sat down to pull on his socks. Holding them in his hand, he said:

'Suppose that a man was just like you say, but he took a pill or something that gave him the strength of ten.'

Isabella got up herself and put on her dressing-gown. She sat at her dressing-table and began brushing out her hair.

She looked at Joe in the mirror. He seemed more than ever like a round-faced baby. She laughed.

'I think Minu's sheltering you a lot too much. Surely, Joe, you know that all that's nonsense. There are no such pills. It's the purest superstition.'

'Yes. But suppose someone invented one. After all, they do wonderful things, today, don't they? I mean the philosopher's stone for changing base metals into gold was a superstition, wasn't it, but Harry tells me it's an accomplished fact today.'

'Well, suppose, then,' said Isabella. 'What then?'

'That's just the point. *What then?* What would happen?'

'I can tell you exactly,' said Isabella, 'because I've been translating a bit about it in my book. Margherita della Quercia did just that thing in 1306. She wasn't a full della Quercia: she came from a collateral branch of the family. She was a bit crazed, poor thing, and fancied herself as a witch. She announced that she had invented a potion which would make men irresistible to women and give them full powers to cope with the situation. In no time at all she was arrested, tried, and Joe, they burned the poor thing at the stake. Of course, witches had been selling love-potions up and down Italy for years – they still do, in fact – and nobody had taken very much notice. But, you see, those were potions for making a man fall in love with *you*, the buyer. No harm was done. But Margherita's potion was a menace to every married woman whose husband might get a chance to buy himself a phial of it. There was a riot of outraged wives in front of the duke's palace. He was forced to jail her and when it came to her trial, the women packed every inch of space in the hall and howled down every sign of mercy on the part of the judges. So she died, God rest her soul. But why do you ask, Joe? Has some wise woman in Salerno sold you a powder made of newts' tails and . . .'

'Let us finish dressing,' said Joe, hastily, 'and go and sit in the garden. It will be beautiful there as the sun goes down.'

So they went and sat together under the oleander tree. Joe asked no more questions. It was, indeed, beautiful at sunset, and a cool breeze rustled the oleander and blew some petals down on them. Later, the moon came up. Joe kissed Isabella. He kissed her again and again. Then he said, in Isabella's ear:

'My darling, I am seized with a general feeling of *bonhomie*, and I feel that I would very much like to wave at a passing train.'

With that, they went indoors again.

PART FIVE

FOUR nights after Harry had begun his hike, the Parliamentary Secretary to the Minister for Agriculture, Andrea Pozzo, was sitting up in bed deploring his fellow-countrymen. This was because he was an Italian of executive ability. He liked to get things done. There are very few such Italians: they are greatly respected by their fellow-countrymen, who spend a great deal of time and thought in seeing to it that they never succeed in getting anything done at all. This is a sort of insurance policy, since in very recent times an Italian with considerable executive ability had to be shot and hung upside down from a lamp-post before he could be stopped doing things. Pozzo had something of this man's drive: he had something, too, of his appearance, for he had a massive head and striking eyes. But he was a much nicer man and far too good for shooting and hanging-upside-down. He had been stopped doing things by the gentler method of being democratically elected to a democratic parliament where, to make things doubly sure, he had been given a post in a democratic government. The dead dictator, from his lamp-post, was no less capable of executive action than Pozzo from his desk in the Ministry.

It was true he had been allowed to set up the laboratory that made the trial sample of Harry's acid. But he had not been given funds to cover the bills. These were now coming in, and Pozzo's memoranda demanding money were going (as the custodian at Paestum could have warned him) from the Ministry of Finance to the Ministry of the Interior, from there to the Ministries of Development, Labour, Transport (there was a garage to be paid for), and Health, and now it rested with the Ministry of Education to get the Ministry's

99

confirmation that the site did not cover the remains of archae-
ological interest.

He was thinking gloomily of how he could explain this to
Harry Wesley, who, with his Anglo-Saxon efficiency, would
not be able to understand so Italian a confusion. Yet he must
be kept happy. Everything now depended on his.figs – everything.

It was then that the telephone rang with the long, shrill
sound reserved for urgent calls from the Ministry.

Pozzo swore and answered:

'Yes?'

'Excellency?'

'Yes.'

'This is the night operator. I have an urgent call for you.'

'Where from?'

'Calabria, Excellency.'

'Who is it?'

'The Englishman, Excellency,' said the operator.

'Pozzo? Is that Pozzo? This is Wesley: Harry Wesley.
Pozzo for God's sake help me.' There was a click as the oper-
ator withdrew himself from the conversation, and then
Harry's voice, high-pitched, his Italian in shambles: 'Pozzo,
I'm . . . Christ, what's the word!'

'Speak English, Mr Wesley. I shall understand. What on
earth has happened?'

'I've been kidnapped.'

'Kidnapped?'

'Yes. By Calabrian bandits. They're standing on either side
of me now. In black hats. Armed. For God's sake do something.'

Pozzo shook the sleep out of his head.

'Mr Wesley. Listen. Can you speak freely?'

'Yes. I think so. They said they'd let me talk to you so
long as they kept me covered.'

'Where are you speaking from?'

'The police station.'

'Good,' said Pozzo. Then, dropping into Italian, he swore again. 'Madonna! What do I mean, "good". Harry, do you mean the police force is conniving at this?'

'There isn't any force. Just one copper. He's a decent chap I think, but they've got him covered, too.'

'How did you get into this mess? No. Don't answer. Tell the policeman to speak to me.'

'All right. Only do something,' said Harry. There was a pause, the sound of men's voices, and then a voice heavy with the accent of Calabria.

'Giovanni Carrano, constable of San Lorenzo, Doctor, at your service.'

Pozzo summoned up all his most official manner. 'You are speaking to the Parliamentary Secretary to the Minister of Agriculture. You will address me as Excellency, without fail.'

A respectful murmur came over the wire.

'Carrano; speak carefully and keep your wits about you. Are you a local gendarme?'

'Yes, Excellency.'

'How big is San Lorenzo?'

'Six hundred souls, Excellency.'

'In the mountains?'

'Right in the mountains, Excellency.'

'Now listen, Carrano. I want you to go to the nearest Carabinieri barracks and ...'

'Excellency, I kiss your feet, but there is no Carabinieri barracks. Two of them come from Potenza.'

'When?'

'Wednesdays and Saturdays.'

'My God,' said Pozzo. 'It is true what the foreigners say about us. We are still in the Middle Ages.'

'Excellency?'

'Never mind. How did this Englishman get into this trouble?'

'He was on a walking tour.'

'Walking! Sometimes I think the roads of England must all be unfit for wheeled traffic, they walk so much.'

'Excellency?'

'Never mind. Who are these bandits? If you cannot answer say "Excellency, the line is bad, I cannot hear you."'

'I can hear Your Excellency's esteemed voice very well,' said the constable. 'They are not bandits. They are my relatives. To be precise, my brother-in-law, my father-in-law, and my wife's cousin. They are respectable people.'

'With guns?'

'Only shot-guns, and they have a licence to hunt, fully paid up and stamped for this year.' There was a pause. 'Yes. Yes. Thank you, Giorgio. Excellency?'

'Yes.'

'They have all just put their hunting licences on the table under my eyes, so I can assure Your Excellency on the bones of St Francesco that they have a right to carry guns.'

'But not to point them at visiting Englishmen in however eccentric a manner he may arrive, even walking.'

'It is not his walking they object to.'

'What is it, then?'

'A thousand apologies for the word,' said the constable, 'but it's his —' The constable used a word in dialect that came ringing through Pozzo's receiver. Pozzo understood it very well, as did every Italian. Pozzo's mouth fell. While he struggled to find something to say, he heard a voice of considerable authority say, in the background, 'Giuseppe, that is no language to use to a gentleman like His Excellency. How many times since you were a little boy have I told you not to use bad words. Give me the telephone before His Excellency reports you for being an ill-educated pig.' Then the voice came nearer and Pozzo heard:

'Excellency, this is Don Ugo Vespasiano. I am the parish priest.'

'Good evening, Don Ugo,' said Pozzo. 'This is His Excellency Doctor Pozzo, Parliamentary Secretary to the Minister of Agriculture. As far as I can gather your parishioners are holding, in defiance of the constitution and to the shame of Italy, a foreigner of English nationality and a scientist of international fame. Will you explain why?'

'Excellency, this is a poor parish and I am a humble priest. You will excuse me if I do not use language suitable to Your Excellency's rank. May the blessed . . .' The priest's voice was lowered in a mumbled prayer, and then, fortified, he said with admirable firmness. 'I did not know that the foreign gentleman was a distinguished scientist, but even scientists are sons of Adam and it is as a son of Adam that he has presented himself to this village. Not to mince matters, Your Excellency, he came walking on his feet all the way from Salerno and asked for food at the house of the worthy family of the Amodios. There he instantly paid court to the daughter of the house, a member of my choir, called Rosa. With this Rosa, he has already spent three nights in pursuits which the Church can only recognize within the bonds of matrimony. Her family are now insisting that he does right by her.'

'Her family?' Pozzo asked. 'You mean the men standing there with guns?'

'They *are* carrying guns,' said the priest. 'But they assure me that they are going hunting.'

'Hunting what?'

'Er . . . quails, Your Excellency.'

'At this time of night?'

'You have to start early to get the best position at sunrise. Quail, as Your Excellency no doubt knows without a humble parish priest telling him, fly out of the rising sun and . . .'

'Don Ugo.'

'Excellency.'

'Is this Rosa married?'

'Thanks be, no, Excellency.'

'Engaged?'

'Yes.'

'To whom?' There was a pause.

'A – well, to somebody. A young man. He does not come to Mass on Sundays. He . . .'

'Where is he now?'

'In the hills. He ran off like a madman, taking his gun with him.'

'Oh, did he? Don Ugo. Which do you, as Rosa's spiritual adviser think that Rosa should marry; the young man in the hills, or this distinguished foreigner?'

'I . . .' said Don Ugo, then stopped. He began again, and once more stopped. 'The foreigner,' he said, with some uncertainty, 'would appear to be well supplied with . . . er . . .'

'Money? Yes.'

'Yes. So I thought. And, of course, he is clearly a gentleman.'

'I am glad you think so.'

'A *Protestant* gentleman,' said Don Ugo, hastily. 'Of course, if he were not a Protestant, I could not overlook his . . . ah . . . precipitate . . . ah . . .' He broke off. 'Excellency,' he said, with a rather pleading sound. 'I would like to consult my bishop about your question.'

'Where is your bishop?'

'Unfortunately he is hundreds of miles away in Ravenna attending a family celebration.'

'Don Ugo,' said Pozzo. 'I would not presume to anticipate your bishop's judgement, but . . . wait a moment. Let me speak to the Englishman.'

In a moment Harry's voice came through:

'Wesley here.'

'Mr Wesley, did you follow what we were saying?'

'More or less,' said Harry, miserably.

'Is it true?'

'More or less.'

'How do you mean?' said Pozzo, sharply. 'Less than three nights. Or more?'

'Pozzo, I cannot possibly discuss this over the telephone. It's a matter of the gravest scientific importance, and as soon as I know all the facts, I shall write a paper on it.'

'Do. Do,' said Pozzo. 'Is she pretty?'

'She might be. I don't know. Yes, she is, I suppose, but . . .'

'So you don't want to marry her?'

'Oh, good God, no! For heaven's sake, Pozzo, don't get any romantic notions about this awful business. You'd be quite, quite wrong,' said Harry, so emphatically that the receiver rattled on Pozzo's ear. 'Just get me out of this mess, and then I'll explain everything. Please, Pozzo, do something.'

'Don't worry, I shall,' said Pozzo. 'Trust me. Now give me the parish priest again.'

When Don Ugo had been brought back to the telephone, Pozzo said:

'As I was saying, Don Ugo, I would not presume to take the place of your bishop, but since he is in Ravenna, what do you think of this solution for our problem? I am now going to telephone Potenza and ask them to send an escort of carabinieri to bring Signor Wesley away. If you will use your influence in your parish to see that all goes smoothly and that nothing happens that might cause scandal, I will personally promise that, from funds at my disposal as Parliamentary Secretary to the Minister of Agriculture, all of Rosa's expenses for her wedding to her young man will be paid by my department, including the price of a new suit for that reprehensible young man who does not go to Mass. What do you think?'

'Well,' said Don Ugo, with the unmistakable tone of a peasant driving a bargain – 'Well, you see . . .'

'And,' said Pozzo, quickly, 'a silver mug for the christening of the first boy *and*,' he waited a moment, 'a donation to the . . . er . . . ah . . .'

'Restoration of the apse,' said Don Ugo, promptly, and then burst into profuse compliments, which ended: 'I thought that such admirable paternal acts on the part of government could have happened only under Fascism.'

'On the contrary,' said Pòzzo, 'the relations of Church and State have never been happier than under our new democratic constitution.'

'It is exactly as Your Excellency is so condescending as to say,' said Don Ugo.

'Well, then, good night, Don Ugo. Please ask the distinguished foreign scientist to speak to me once again for I must tell him of what we have arranged.'

'Immediately, Your Excellency. It has been an honour to speak to Your Excellency.'

'It has been a pleasure to speak to so understanding a person as yourself, Monsignor. You *are* a Monsignor, no doubt?'

'No, Excellency.'

'Ah,' said Pozzo, and put all the mysterious power of those in office into his voice. 'I must speak to my uncle His Eminence Silvio Cardinal Capuano. Good night, Don Vespasiano. Good night and thank you.'

Pozzo briefly explained his plan to Harry. He replaced the receiver. He leaned back among the pillows and mopped his forehead. He felt pleased with himself. The Englishman had demanded action, and, in a twinkling, Pozzo had acted. He had bought the Englishman out of his trouble.

Then he remembered that there were no funds and he groaned aloud.

*

'And now,' said Don Ugo, turning majestically to the company, 'we shall go to my house and I shall tell those whom it concerns what His Excellency, the Parliamentary Secretary to the Minister of Agriculture, has said, from Rome, to me. You, you, and you, come with me,' he said to the men with guns. 'And,' he added, turning to Harry, 'if you will honour my humble house with your presence, sir, I would take it as a very great compliment.'

Don Ugo was tall; he had cropped grey hair; and his face was usually flushed red with exasperation at the ways of his parishioners. He treated them much as a sergeant-major treats his troops, except that he plainly had little hope that they would obey him. He treated Harry, on the other hand, with worldly courtesy.

A girl of remarkable ugliness who was, it would appear, Don Ugo's servant, was sent scurrying ahead. Don Ugo took Harry's arm and the three men in black hats fell in behind with the constable. Don Ugo turned to the crowd which surrounded them. 'Nobody else,' he said, 'and if I catch anybody listening at the windows, there will be no band at next week's *festa*. I shall send the money to the missionaries.' His face flushed a deeper red. 'I *can*, you know,' he said, and with that marched himself and Harry to his house, taking long strides that made the skirts of his soutane whistle.

The house was very small. The living-room had walls on which the damp had made huge patterns. It was unfurnished save for straight-back chairs with wooden seats, a wooden cupboard, and a large table. This, to Harry's astonishment, was of the flashiest contemporary design, with metal legs and a transparent glass top. Don Ugo patted it.

'Do you like it, signor?' he said to Harry.

Harry said it was in the very latest taste.

'So the shopkeeper told me,' said Don Ugo, with satisfaction.

Don Ugo had begun moving the chairs towards it when the eldest man with the gun, who was Rosa's father, and who had laid aside neither his gun nor his hat on entering, said:

'The cloth, if you please, Don Ugo.'

Don Ugo's face flushed again.

'The cloth,' he repeated, bitterly. 'The cloth.' He blew contemptuously down his nose and then bellowed, 'Marta, the cloth.'

The servant-girl scuttled in immediately, carrying a large white tablecloth which she hastily spread and smoothed over the glass top of the table.

'You,' said Don Ugo to Harry, 'being a man of taste and education, like my table. My parishioners say it gives them rheumatism in their elbows and spoils their shooting. Although I should have thought that the amount of my wine they drink at it would have kept out bubonic plague, let alone rheumatism.' He said this quite unsmilingly, but the three men laughed heartily and put their shot-guns against the wall. As a further gesture towards good manners, they pushed their hats off their foreheads on to the backs of their heads.

There was now a great to-do about who should sit at the head of the table, all refusing until Harry, who would have wished to have been in the darkest corner of the room, such was his embarrassment, found himself presiding over the company.

The servant-girl brought red wine which was poured into thick glasses. All, including the father of the girl he had seduced, politely drank his health. Don Ugo then began, in a dialect which Harry could barely follow, to explain His Excellency's proposition.

*

Harry gulped his wine and misery welled up in him.

'Two,' he said to himself. 'Level-pegging. But God knows what Joe's notched up since I left him.'

It had happened so suddenly. He had been feeling free from the monstrous thing and then he had asked for some food at a farm. Rosa had served it. He had looked at her, in her thin dress. He had looked so hard and so long that she bent over him and kissed him on the top of his head. 'Naughty!' she had whispered. 'Naughty handsome Englishman.'

He had made a tremendous, wrenching effort of will.

'Is there,' he had said, 'anything of historical interest in this place?'

Rosa had replied:

'Yes. The olive grove. At three o'clock. Everybody will be taking their afternoon sleep.'

She had then gone to the door and, turning, she had given him a look of abandoned love.

He had kept the tryst, three quarters of an hour early.

They had gone back to her house, and Rosa had insisted that he stay. There was no public place to stay in the tiny village, so he was given, cheerfully enough, the room which touring officials used who did not want to stay with the priest. Two more afternoons had been spent in the olive grove and then he had returned with Rosa to find the men with the guns. He could not blame them. Rosa had made no secret of her infatuation for him, ogling him at meals, lingering by his side, sighing, and worse, glowing with pride in the evenings. When she had seen her father and brother and cousin with their shot-guns, she had screamed, pushed past them, and run into the kitchen. She had come out almost immediately with her hair streaming, her eyes wild, and a carving-knife in her hand. But the ease with which her mother, a frail, small woman, had disarmed her, persuaded Harry that guns were not as much of a surprise to her as they were to him. 'I love him,' she had screamed. 'If I do not marry him, I shall kill myself and kill all of the rest of you at the same time.' It was the first time that Harry had heard the word 'marriage'. He was to hear it a great many more times until, the constable having been called, he had shown

Pozzo's letter as evidence of his identity, and insisted that Pozzo be reached on the telephone. Hours later, the call had come through.

It seemed that Pozzo had done the right thing, because the men round the table, still speaking their barely comprehensible dialect, were grinning at him, raising their glasses, and generally giving every sign of satisfaction.

At last they got up, took their guns, and each shaking Harry's hand effusively, went out of the house.

*

When the men had gone away, Don Ugo said:

'Sit down, Mr Wesley, and let us have a glass of wine together in peace. First, let us take off this ridiculous tablecloth. There, that's better. Now we can be comfortable. I have arranged for a bed to be made up for you here, if you will do me the honour of sleeping the night.' Seeing that Harry was about to speak, Don Ugo added, firmly: 'Putting aside false courtesies, I must tell you that it is quite essential that you do me the honour of sleeping here. If you sleep anywhere else, Rosa's fiancé will shoot you – before he has had time to hear of our little arrangement with His Excellency. Whereas here,' said Don Ugo, pouring out two more glasses of the heavy red wine, 'in my own house, you will almost certainly be safe. After thirteen years of slaving in this parish I will not claim that I have taught them that to shoot a man is wrong, but I think that I have taught them that to shoot him in their parish priest's house is disrespectful.'

'I'm sure you have,' said Harry. 'As far as I can see, you are the only man they do respect here.'

'I manage to scare them, sometimes,' Don Ugo admitted. 'I've got such a terrible temper. The priest who was here before me was a sweet, kind, Christian soul, who loved his neighbours even if they were the pack of scoundrels, contraband runners, drunkards, fornicators, and thieves that are in this village. He moved one of the dozen heathen images which they worship here under the names of good Catholic saints. So they locked him out of his own church and chased him from the village with dogs. The bishop had heard of my terrible temper, so he asked me to take over. He said, frankly, that he was sending me because he thought the villagers had thoroughly deserved me. Besides,' said Don Ugo, putting back his shoulders, 'I am a few centimetres taller than any other man in the place.'

'You must have had a hard time keeping order in the place,' said Harry. He looked at his reflection in the table-top and an idea began forming in his mind. He wondered for a moment how he could approach the matter with Don Ugo, and then said, 'How do you do it, Father? I mean, I suppose, since they're all Catholics, they have to come and confess their sins to you?'

'Only if I've found out beforehand what they've been up to: and I usually do. In that case I simply refuse to sign the good conduct certificates they want to get their gun licences until they come and confess themselves properly.'

'Anything,' said Harry, slowly, 'that is confessed to you is, of course, a secret, isn't it?'

'Oh no!' said Don Ugo, promptly. 'I always make a point of that in my Easter sermon. "If any of you," I say, "comes to me and tells me that you've committed murder, remember, my son, that it is my duty and privilege to go straight to the telephone and ring up the carabinieri, just like any other honest citizen who wears trousers instead of a soutane. That," I tell them, "is the law, both of the Church and the State."'

'But anything else is secret?'

'Yes.'

'What happens if someone confesses some very unusual sin?'

'Fortunately my parishioners aren't a very original lot.

But if it happens say in a city parish, we priests just turn up the book.' He pointed to a row of books on top of the cupboard and then, seeing his guest's interest, he got up and took a fat paper-bound volume from the row. He banged the dust out of it, saying, 'You see what I mean?' and handed it to Harry.

Harry opened the book, thumbed through the pages and saw, in the analytical table of contents at the end, a perspective of human vices that earned his admiration. Then he said slowly:

'Father, I have, I think, committed a sin which is so new that you won't find it even in this thick book.'

Don Ugo smiled as benignly as his stern features allowed. 'No, no, Mr Wesley, that is impossible. You are a Protestant, I believe. Protestants do not admit sin, so you cannot have committed one.'

'I think Protestants do admit sin,' said Harry. 'Indeed they do.'

'No,' said Don Ugo, beginning to flush, 'excuse me but they do not. Why do you think Luther and those others fought all those terrible wars? They certainly didn't go to all that trouble and danger to be sinners like us Catholics. What would they have gained? No, Mr Wesley, you are fortunate in *not* having committed a sin, although perhaps you feel that you have offended against your code as a *gentleman*,' he said, saying the word in English. 'That I know is the English Protestants' substitute for sin, and very good I think it, too. Very good, indeed. Only it wouldn't do for us Italians. We are too hot-blooded. So we stay Catholics. Have some more wine.'

'Whether I can sin or not,' said Harry, quietly and seriously, 'may I tell you what it is I have done?'

Don Ugo did not answer for a moment. He looked at his guest curiously.

'I feel that I must tell somebody or else go off my head,' said Harry, in the same earnest tone.

'Then by all means, tell me,' said Don Ugo. 'Just a moment. I will get some biscuits and then we can drink and eat and you can talk and I shall listen.'

When the biscuits had been put on the table, Harry said:

'First, I must tell you what my work is.'

That done, Harry told him about the fig tree. Thus Don Ugo, a parish priest in a remote mountain village deep in the south of Italy, became the first person to learn of the strange experience of Harry and Joe.

Don Ugo listened attentively. From time to time he asked questions. When he understood that the experience could happen to anyone who ate the fruit, he nodded vigorously, as though he had foreseen this. When Harry had finished his story, he said to Don Ugo,

'So there. I think you'll agree that it's a moral problem that's not to be found in books.'

'Not that one,' said Don Ugo, pointing to the manual. 'But that's only meant for parish priests. But in Rome, in the Vatican, there is a large palace called the Holy Office. It's run by a cardinal: a very powerful man he is, too. Now the job of the Holy Office is to advise the Holy Father on what is right and what is wrong.'

'A big job,' said Harry.

Don Ugo nodded. 'They've been doing it for centuries, which makes it easier,' he said. 'A Jesuit friend of mine once told me that a few years ago when the question of artificial insemination came up, they turned to their files and found they had settled the whole thing in the seventeenth century. I can quite see why you're worried . . .'

'I'm worried about what I should do as the responsible person,' said Harry.

'. . . and what I advise you to do is to go and talk to them.

You won't get to see the cardinal. He's too grand. But you could talk to one of the monsignors. And,' said Don Ugo, heartily, 'the splendid thing is that since you're a Protestant, you needn't take the slightest notice of what you're told. We poor Catholics have to.'

Soon after that they went to bed. In the morning the carabinieri came to escort Harry to safety. They were most respectful. A mile from the village they drew up their car, and one of them got down and opened the door for Harry to get out. Harry looked through the window and saw Rosa, standing tearfully by the wayside for a farewell kiss. The carabinieri were surprised and not a little scandalized when Harry brusquely told them to drive on.

'The English,' one said to the other, and the other sighed dramatically.

*

Harry took no notice of them. He took no notice of Rosa, who by cutting across country, managed to wave a final and desperate appeal at a bend in the road. He took no notice of the scenery. He took no notice of anything whatever because he was deep in thought.

He was thinking, with an intensity he had not known before, about the palace, where a cardinal settled what was right and what was wrong, in the Vatican. By the time he got home he had made up his mind that he would go there.

PART SIX

CARDINALS are priests. They wear scarlet (which is called *the purple*); they rank with princes of the blood, and they are addressed as 'Your Eminence'. They are most august persons. In Italy, you may not be rude to one. It is called 'insulting the Empurpled Ones', and it may land you in jail.

However, there are cardinals and cardinals. There are the run-of-the-mill Eminences; these hold Sees that traditionally have been ruled by cardinals, and so when they become Archbishops, in due course the Pontiff sends them a cardinal's hat. These only come to the Vatican when the occasion calls for it. But there are some Empurpled Ones who are more deeply dyed, as it were, than the rest. These are the cardinals who work in the Vatican, and they are the most august of all. Even among these there are grades, and the most august of the most august, the Eminence of Eminences, was, at this time, the cardinal who ran the Holy Office that Don Ugo had recommended to Harry. This cardinal's name was Rezzonico.

Don Ugo had never seen him. Don Ugo had never, in fact, so much as kissed the ring of any of the Curia cardinals, as these Eminences who run the Vatican are called. He had only seen them from a distance, and distance lends awe to a cardinal, who does not, in truth, need to borrow much of it. Don Ugo held the Curia in the profoundest respect, as do most priests outside the Vatican and even some inside it. For all that, he was responsible for the cardinals of the Curia receiving the most subtle and effective of insults hurled at the Empurpled Ones since the roaring days of the nineteenth century, when they were sometimes pelted in the streets.

Three days after Harry drove away with his escort of carabinieri, each of the cardinals of the Curia received a present.
It was a large basket, heavily gilded and tied round with a
scarlet satin bow. Each basket was labelled with the full titles
of a Curia cardinal, beautifully hand-written on a vellum
tag. The titles ran into several lines. The baskets contained
figs.

They were good figs – not Harry's, but good. There was no
indication of where they came from, and the donor did not
give his name. Had the anonymous joker thrown the figs one
by one at Their Eminences' scarlet robes, he could not have
created a greater effect, because on the evening they arrived
Harry's and Joe's secret had been published to the world.

*

This was the work of a young man who lived in a town in
the mountains a few miles from Don Ugo's parish. He
wanted to become a writer. He had managed to persuade the
editor of a newspaper of extreme left-wing views to let him
cover the area of his home town and the surrounding hills.
Since nothing ever happened in these localities except mur-
ders, it was arranged that he should be paid per murder per
column-centimetre published, including headlines. This
worked out well enough when the murder was done with a
hatchet, for the headline writers liked the word and spread
themselves. But mere shootings barely covered his lunch and
his shoe-leather.

He was, therefore, always on the alert for a story that
would be published and yet would not concern lowly paid
homicide. He heard of Harry almost as soon as he arrived,
but he did not know that he was a celebrated man. This was
because nobody in Southern Italy troubles to remember anybody's second name unless it is a nickname such as One-leg,
or Crooked-back or Dirty. Thus the young journalist heard
only that a signor Arrigo had stayed at a village. Then he

heard that Signor *Arrigo* had been escorted out of the area by two carabinieri. He immediately went to the village and straight to Don Ugo.

Don Ugo was, at first, reluctant to tell the young man anything. He admitted there had been some trouble with the villagers. He agreed that Harry had gone away under escort, but a perfectly honourable one. Thus far, he said, he would go, but further he would not. His definite manner of saying this instantly told the young reporter that there was something remarkable in the wind.

Instead of cross-questioning Don Ugo, the young man merely said that he was a local boy who had never murdered anybody and did not want to. He was earning an honest living by the sweat of his brow, he said, just as his parish priest had always told him he should. Then he silently showed Don Ugo his frayed cuffs, his empty wallet, and, lastly, the holes in each of his shoes.

Don Ugo's heart melted. Here, indeed, was evidence that it is the wicked who flourish like the green bay tree, and not the good. He thought the matter over. After all, Harry had not bound him to secrecy (Harry had thought it unnecessary. Were not priests automatically bound?) Further, Harry had not confessed. He had not been on his knees. He had not said the prescribed words. Don Ugo had not been wearing his stole. Finally – and here the stern lips of Don Ugo broke into a broad and satisfied laugh – Harry was a Protestant.

He invited the young man to share his midday spaghetti, and, over it, he told all he could remember.

The things he had forgotten or had not quite understood were easily found out. When the young journalist returned, hot-foot, to his house, he found full biographies of Harry in the back files of the newspaper, together with descriptions of Pozzo's laboratory and of the opening ceremony.

He debated with himself whether he should go and interview Harry. But there were two good reasons against it. He had not got the bus fare for the long journey down the mountain and round the bay : and secondly, he might be scooped. He wrote his piece, put it in an envelope and posted it (for in Italy circulations are small and the telephone expensive) in the box on the next express train leaving Potenza for Rome.

He had put all the skill he had into his story and it was well done. But still it might not have been published. The editor of the newspaper was a man of systematic opinions. There were things he was for and there were things he was against. He was against America, priests, and big cars. He was for Russia, scientists, and low-priced motor-scooters within reach of the working classes. In his newspaper, motor-scooters were never in the wrong in the respect of a road accident, and scientists (even if they were American) were never immoral. His experience was that to break such rules as these only confused his loyal readers; and it was his belief that when it was necessary to confuse his readers, it should always be done in an editorial. The young man's piece might therefore have gone into the wastepaper basket, save for one thing.

Italian newspapers are verbosely reluctant to come to the point, like their readers. A good story is always begun with a long preamble, working all round the subject or narrating its background. The news comes at the bottom of the second column. The preambles are greatly enjoyed, and that is the reason why Italy is one of the few countries in Europe where one may see men finishing their morning's newspaper in the stalls at the Opera.

The young journalist's preamble had been a vivid description of the scene of Pozzo's laboratory being blessed by a cardinal.

The editor, although he was for scientists, was heavily against cardinals. He read to the finish. He telephoned for his leader-writer. He talked to his leader-writer for half an hour. Then he put on his hat and went to a fashionable fruit

shop, and gave a large order, under an assumed name, which
he paid for in cash.

*

The Vatican is a small park in Rome, lying behind the Basilica of St Peter's and surrounded by a wall. It contains some
large buildings and two palaces, one of which is small and is
occupied by the Governor of the Vatican, the second being
large and the home of the Pope, who is usually the supreme
master of the whole place.

But at the time that these events took place he was not;
or at least he was its master only in name, because he lay
sick with an obstinate and exhausting illness that had kept
him to his bed for many months. His illness was a cause of
sorrow to multitudes, both those of his faith and those who
did not share it, for all the world held him to be a great and
good man. Had he played any part in the events of which I
am writing, things would have been different. But he did
not. He was not even told of them, for it was essential that
he should not be disturbed or worried. He lay, reverently
tended and guarded from any intrusion, in his summer
palace on the Alban Hills, where, it was hoped, the purer air
would aid his recovery.

*

Thus the Vatican was run, at this time, by the Curia cardinals. There were only five of them, for the Pope had been
too ill to replace those who had died. Of these five, one was in
charge of the office of the Propaganda of the Faith and had
little to do with the rest of the work of the Vatican, and one,
as we shall see, was on the shelf. Of the three remaining,
none had the energy, the brains, and the authority of Rezzonico, who from the Holy Office ran the whole place.

The newspaper carrying the young journalist's story of
Harry (with an editorial comment) was available at midnight. By seven in the morning, all five of the cardinals of
the Curia had received their figs. Rezzonico's were delivered

119

to the Holy Office, which is just outside the walls of the Vatican. They were taken in by the porter and sent straight to the monsignor who was Rezzonico's secretary. The others were delivered to the Gate of St Anne, which is large and guarded by Switzers, but which is, in fact, the Vatican's tradesmen's entrance, where they were collected in due course by the cardinals' servants.

The most piquant of these gifts was, of course, the one intended for Silvio Cardinal Capuano, because he had blessed the laboratory and was Pozzo's uncle. This basket, which was especially fine and equipped with an elaborate handle, was received by Maria.

*

Maria was a 'Perpetua': that is to say she was a woman who devotes her life to looking after a priest. She makes his meals, she cleans his house, she darns his socks, and she listens to his troubles. She had looked after Silvio Capuano from the day he had come to her parish to be the parish priest, when he had taken up his quarters in two rooms no bigger nor more splendid than Don Ugo's. She had looked after him when he had been in charge of a seminary and he had lived in an apartment. She had been his housekeeper when he had been made a bishop and lived in a large house. She had continued to be his housekeeper when he had been elevated to an archbishopric and lived in a vast and ancient palace. She was still his 'Perpetua' now that he was a cardinal. But once more she had only two rooms to look after, for Capuano was the cardinal who had been put on the shelf.

Maria knew this quite well. It merely deepened her devotion to him. Maria was not awed by the Vatican. To the world, it is a mysterious place which governs by spiritual authority alone the religious life of one seventh of the human race. To Maria it was another parish, another seminary, another diocese. That is to say, it was a place where her master worked among a number of other priests, most of whom, in her opinion, were only out to make trouble and difficulties for him.

On the morning that the figs were delivered she woke at six, and as she had done for fifty years, she said her prayers and washed her face. She then knocked on the Cardinal's bedroom door to wake him so that he could go and say his daily mass on time. She tidied the main room of the apartment. When she heard her master go downstairs and close the front door behind him, she watched out of the window as he walked to the chapel. Satisfied that he was well and no slower or more bowed than usual, she set about getting him his morning coffee. There was no kitchen, so she opened a cupboard and took out a large battered thermos-flask which she put into a shopping-bag. She left the building in which she lived, and walked along the asphalt paths of the Vatican, in the vast morning shadow of St Peter's. She took no notice of the church, because she was silently reciting the rosary, her thin lips moving with the words. It was a rosary with her own improvements; before each of the meditations she inserted a request that Capuano should pass the day happily and in peace of mind, 'because, you know,' she said silently, 'he is a saint.' Without interrupting her thoughts or her prayers, she said 'Good morning' to a gendarme, nodded to a pale-faced young Swiss Guard who was yawning and rubbing sleep out of his eyes, and finished her recitation just as she arrived at the Vatican. There the man behind the bar gave her a small cup of black coffee, which she drank herself, sipping it slowly not for her own refreshment but to make sure the coffee in the urn was to the Cardinal's taste. When she was satisfied that it was, she handed the battered thermos-flask to the man behind the bar, who filled it for her.

Then she bought some bread, which she put together with the battered thermos into the black bag.

She was walking back to the long tawny building where

the Cardinal had his quarters when somebody came running after her and gave her the basket of fruit. When she was quite sure that the handsome gift was really for Capuano, tears came to her eyes. It was a long time since anybody, who was not of his own family, had sent him a present. Curia cardinals are quickly forgotten when they are dead. One of them, to remind himself of the fact, arranged that he should be buried under the floor of his own church, and that his memorial should be of marble slab no more than twelve inches long and four inches wide – big enough, that is, to carry his name and nothing more. The same oblivion can overtake a Curia cardinal when he is still alive, if by ill-luck he has fallen out of favour. Thus Maria, who did not read newspapers, was overjoyed with the gilded basket and bore it in triumph to her master.

'Look, Don Silvio,' she cried (for she had never changed his title since the first day she had worked for him), 'someone has sent you a beautiful present. There's no name – but isn't it lovely?'

He got up from his seat by the window. Maria thought how more and more like a saint he looked as he grew older, with his silver hair, his pale, soft skin, and his tranquil eyes. He took the basket, and he smiled with pleasure.

'And I was feeling rather sad this morning,' he said to Maria. 'I was sitting in the window, wondering what I was going to do with the rest of the day. Now who could it be, do you think, who's sent it?'

*

According to the pontifical annual, His Eminence should have been a busy man. For the last three years he had been the cardinal in charge of what the annual called the Reverend Fabric. That is the vast stone pile of St Peter's Basilica. On the first day of his appointment to the post he had gone round the church with the superintending engineer. He had made a suggestion for repairs. The next day the engineer called on him. With profound respects and the aid of some beautifully executed drawings, the engineer explained to His Eminence that His Eminence's suggestion would cost approximately a half a million dollars and probably bring down the dome. Then Capuano knew for certain what he had feared for some time. He had not been given a new job. He had been put out to grass.

He had borne his dismissal with humble resignation. He was, as Maria believed, a good Christian. Indeed, being a good Christian had earned him the red hat, or so it was said. When he had come to the Vatican, the monsignors had nick-named him 'the missionary' becauses it was rumoured that the Holy Father, plagued by factions among the cardinals, had brought him to the Vatican to evangelize the Sacred Col-lege and bring it back to the Faith. His fellow-cardinals quickly saw that he was indeed a saint, and after due thought they found him a task that only a saint could do. Each of the cardinals was the nominal patron of a long roster of orders of nuns and holy women. It was agreed that when the abbesses and mother-superiors came to the Vatican with their troubles, they should be told to take them to Cardinal Capuano. His Eminence laboured, or rather listened, for five years. Then his health collapsed under the strain. He lay sick for several months and when he recovered he found him-self the cardinal in charge of the Reverend Fabric. Cardinal Capuano had freely admitted that he was a failure. But Maria would not. According to Maria, the whole thing was an intrigue of Rezzonico's.

*

Rezzonico's post as the chief of the palace where right and wrong was settled suited him very well. He had the figure for it. He was tall; he was commanding; he had a large and opinionated nose. He wore his purple as one born to it, and, in a sense, he was.

The small boys of the North Italian town in which he had

been born were fond of playing at funerals. Whenever Rezzonico's turn had come to conduct the ceremony, he always refused to be a mere parish priest and insisted on being a bishop. One day a real bishop, taking a stroll in the street, had come across Rezzonico and his companions at play. Rezzonico was wearing a paper mitre, and he was burying a cat. As soon as they saw the bishop, Rezzonico and his companions had immediately taken to their heels. But on the bishop's insistence they had been brought back, and Rezzonico had been made to go through with the rest of the ceremony. The real bishop was so impressed with what he had seen that he called the boy to his palace. He questioned him closely. A year later, he sent Rezzonico to the best seminary in the area and paid his fees until he became a priest.

The rector of this seminary told the bishop that his protégé had done very well. He had shown great gifts. He had stood first in Latin, in History, and in Theology. As for mathematics, in forty years of teaching the rector had never seen any boy so apt.

The rector was less happy about his spiritual attainments. Rezzonico, said the rector, could write a Ciceronian essay on humility without, the rector felt, knowing in the least what it was. In his theological exercises, he could take both sides of the dispute with equal facility and equal brilliance, but, in all his time in the seminary, he had never once been known to admit he was wrong. He was able to do calculations in his head with astonishing rapidity, but while some people who have this gift seem almost unaware of it, nobody could say that about Rezzonico. His morals were above reproach. There was not a black mark against him. It seemed (the rector summed up) that the Devil, like everybody else in the seminary, had respectfully kept his distance. The rector, however, was fundamentally a cheerful man and he told the bishop that a few years as assistant priest in a poor parish among very humble people would teach Rezzonico the principles of truly holy living, which the rector said he felt he had been unable to do.

The bishop replied that it was one of the glories of the Church that she never lacked priests who lived holy lives, but in his experience priests with a head for figures were as rare as rain in the Sahara. He needed such a man himself. So, then and there, Rezzonico was appointed by the bishop to be an assistant to his Vicar-general, with the task of re-organizing the diocesan finances.

Rezzonico knew that this was his great chance in life, and prayerfully he took it with both hands. After a week of studying the diocesan accounts, he had gone straight to the heart of the matter. He saw that the real trouble was that the bishop could not do long-division, and invented every excuse in order to avoid having to try. Within a month the bishop had learned to lean upon the brilliant young priest in every question involving arithmetic. Within a year, a neighbouring bishop tried to steal his services; within two, the neighbouring bishop had succeeded. Soon Rezzonico had invented a system of book-keeping which could be under-stood by bishops, and yet balanced. The second bishop yielded to the entreaties of a third bishop, the third to the pleas of a fourth, and thus Rezzonico was passed on from diocese to diocese, leaving behind him golden opinions and money in the till. Inevitably, so rare a man was called to the Vatican.

But here he found a discipline sterner than any that his rector had recommended. His gifts were appreciated; his influence increased; but for twenty years he owned to no higher title than that of a monsignor. This entitled him to a salute from the Swiss Guard, but to very little else. He knew he was indispensable: but he was martyred by the prelates who knew it too.

He practised the Christian virtues of patience, humility, and self-abnegation in the ante-rooms of the Vatican until he had a character like steel. It helped him to keep up with his studies. Having nothing else to do while he waited, he read books on theology, science, history, and politics – books which other priests were too busy even to open. Noticing that the hierarchy hardly ever read newspapers, he studied them assiduously by the hour and soon became the best informed man on the place. Tours of duty abroad in Europe and America had added to his knowledge of the world and his power in the Vatican. By the time he was sixty he had to give up his studies, because nobody any longer dared to keep him waiting. When the offer of a cardinal's hat came, he had at first refused it on the grounds that it would not suit a man who had spent his life in such a humble capacity. But since this humble capacity consisted, as everybody well knew, in having run most of the Vatican for a decade from behind the scenes, nobody took this very seriously. After a decent interval, he bowed to Authority and, at last, consented to put on the purple. Never had it fitted a man better.

While sitting in ante-chambers he had discovered that the only thing that can be perceived clearly through a closed door are the shortcomings of the man inside. As a young priest he had been astonished to find bishops who could not do long-division; as an old man he was barely surprised to find cardinals who could do nothing at all. Maria, was therefore, wrong. Rezzonico had not actually intrigued against his brother-cardinal. He was certain he was a fool; but he agreed that he might be a saint.

The Vatican is governed by the Sacred Congregations, which are a series of committees of cardinals and others. While Capuano had been ill, Rezzonico had reorganized them. He had suggested Capuano's name charitably for those Sacred Congregations which hardly ever met. To show his respect for Capuano's spiritual qualities, he, by what he considered a rather happy stroke, had suggested Capuano for the duties of looking after the Reverend Fabric, a post which had been vacant for several years. It conjured up a picture in his vivid mind of the old man ending his days in the vast basilica, shuffling round it, respected by all, and lovingly ordering the stuccoes to be restored. Besides, there was the competent superintendent to see that he could do no harm, such as spending too much money; nor come to any, such as falling off ladders.

*

That settled, Rezzonico forgot him, like everybody else, until the day when the cardinals got their figs. Then he telephoned him. Capuano was sipping his coffee, looking out of the window and nodding his head gently at nothing in particular; Maria was chatting about the figs, when suddenly they were both startled by the sound of the telephone bell, a call, these days, being a most unusual event.

The instrument was at the other end of the room, so to save her master trouble Maria went and answered it. She lifted the receiver and bellowed, 'Pronto! Pronto! Pronto!' with the full force of her lungs. She did this because that is how people had answered the telephone fifty years before in her country town, and she had seen no reason to change.

Rezzonico, at the other end of the line, held the instrument away from his ear and looked across his splendid desk at Monsignor Di Pino, his secretary. 'He still uses the instrument,' he said, shaking his head sadly, 'like a peasant telephoning for a veterinary surgeon to cure a sick cow.' He uncovered the mouthpiece again.

'Is that Cardinal Capuano?' he said, respectfully lowering his voice.

'No,' said Maria. 'This is Maria.'

The Cardinal changed his tone.

'I wish to speak to His Eminence,' he said. 'And this is Rezzonico.'

Maria tightened her lips.

'His Eminence is in the bathroom,' she said. Her voice was every bit as firm as the Cardinal's. The receiver clattered in her ear, but she was not listening. She gently replaced it in its bracket.

Capuano said:

'Who was that?'

'Rezzonico.'

Capuano rose shakily to his feet in alarm.

'Why did you say I was in the bathroom?' he said, greatly agitated.

'To give you time to think,' said Maria.

'Think? But what about?'

Tears came into Maria's old grey eyes.

'About whatever it is that you have done wrong,' she said.

'But Maria,' the Cardinal protested, 'I'm not a parish priest being telephoned by his bishop. I'm ...'

At that moment the telephone rang again, and this time Capuano answered it. There was an exchange of courtesies and then for a time the rattle of Rezzonico's voice.

'I shall come and see you straight away,' said Capuano.

There were polite protestations from the other end of the telephone, but finally Capuano had his way. He put down the phone slowly. He turned to Maria.

'You were right,' he said.

*

He told Maria to send for his car and went into his bedroom. As all the world knows, cardinals dress very splendidly. The robes, the skirt, the cross, the ring, the hat, are most magnificent in their effect. Kings have spent long hours endeavouring to design for themselves a uniform that would outshine that of a cardinal in full state, but they have never succeeded. But there are times when a cardinal wishes to be modest. Then he dresses in sober black save for red piping round the button-holes of his soutane, a red stock, red stockings and a gold and scarlet band around his hat. The splendour is still there but only glimpsed, like the noonday sun, through the slats of a Venetian blind. It can be gazed upon, but borne. A full range of these princely accessories hung in the cupboards of Capuano's bedroom. Some of them were a little shabby: the shops that sell them near the Pantheon are expensive and Capuano was not rich. Still, they were serviceable: but he did not take them off their hangers. Instead, he peered into the small mirror and combed his hair. He brushed some specks off his ordinary black soutane, took his plain round hat off a peg and smoothed its furry surface with his sleeve. He put the hat on his head carefully and squarely, looking in the miror to see that it was right. He stood by his bedroom door for a moment, thinking what else was needed to fit him for the encounter. He looked down at his shoes, and with a little cry of dismay he saw that they were dusty. He lifted the skirts of his soutane and, balancing himself a little precariously, he rubbed the toe of each against the back of his black socks. This done, he felt he was quite ready. Hearing the sound of the car on the gravel outside his front-door, he went downstairs.

Two visiting nuns, seeing the small man in the back of the long black car, thought that he was a parish priest being given a ride by some indulgent prelate. They were astonished to find that when the little parish priest was driven past the sentries he was greeted with a crash of salutes. The car drove a little way, then drew up at the gate of the palazzo where Rezzonico worked.

Here, he was received with every requirement of the protocol that governs the visit of cardinals to one another. The ritual monsignor stood outside in the sun: other monsignors made a ritual dash from the shadows of the doorway as soon as the car came to a halt. Capuano's ring was kissed with the required sweeping genuflections. He was conducted along the corridors with a rustle of soutanes like the wind among autumn leaves.

When he was ushered into the Cardinal's room, Rezzonico

rose from his chair like the sun. He was in full panoply: scarlet silk and white lace billowed away from his large frame, while the great gold cross which hung from his neck on a golden chain swung rhythmically in time with his stately progress round his enormous walnut desk. Their Eminences met: they touched hands. The room was large and lined with red damask, and as Rezzonico led his guest down the length of it to his chair, Their Eminences chatted. It is perhaps surprising that cardinals are masters of small talk, but on the great occasions of the Church, cardinals are seen together in public and they are minutely observed. They must be seen and heard to talk: they must appear to be friendly, and they must say nothing of any consequence whatsoever. There were many people in the big room, so now the two cardinals, as they walked towards their chairs, smiled at each other and made conversation. Capuano apologized for his old soutane. Rezzonico apologized for his own splendour. He was, he said, due at a ceremony in an hour.

Capuano said:

'I envy Your Eminence's busy life.'

Rezzonico said:

'I envy Your Eminence's peace and quiet. I don't think it good for a priest to be as busy as I am, and one day I intend to do as you do.'

Capuano said:

'I hope not. Two cardinals interfering with his work would be more than the superintendent could bear.'

The monsignors laughed, but Rezzonico smiled very briefly. It is permissible for cardinals to joke about themselves in public, but this joke had too much edge to it to be quite proper. It was, Rezzonico reflected, as they walked down the room, characteristic of the whole man. He was modest and self-deprecating, with just that little touch of excess which never failed to put him in the centre of the picture. It was permissible, for instance, for cardinals to go about the Vatican plainly dressed. In fact it was encouraged. But as Rezzonico noticed, running his eye over Capuano's soutane, his brother-cardinal's dress was so plain that it had all the éclat of sackcloth and ashes. Rezzonico decided that it was time that they were alone. He nodded to Di Pino. For a while the room was filled with a susurration of monsignors as they genuflected, kissed rings, took their leave, and left the room. Only Di Pino remained behind.

'Let us go over and sit on the couch. We shall be more comfortable,' said Rezzonico, adding to Di Pino, 'Please telephone for some coffee.'

The two prelates sat in either corner of a vast couch, while Di Pino whispered into the telephone. That done, the monsignor took his seat modestly on a hard chair in the background.

*

Rezzonico put his hands to his face, and drew them down slowly, massaging his eye-balls as he did so. He sighed deeply, snuffing up a great volume of air, through his opinionated nose. Then he said:

'Now for this most unfortunate business. I scarcely know where to start.'

'With me it's best to start at the very beginning,' said Capuano. 'People are always surprised by the amount of things that I don't know. You said over the telephone that it was about that factory I blessed.'

'Laboratory,' corrected Rezzonico.

'That's right. So it was.'

'Have you seen this morning's newspaper?' said Rezzonico.

'No.'

'Or yesterday's?'

'No.'

'Nor the day's before, I suppose?'

'Not even that,' said Capuano, apologetically. 'To tell you

the truth, I don't read the newspapers at all. There you are, you see. I've shocked you already. I hope you don't think it's remiss of me. With you it's quite different. With all the irons you've got in ... that is to say, with the vast range of things you have to deal with, it must be quite necessary. But I've found the newspapers don't help me much in my job. After all, if the dome of St Peter's fell down in the night, I should hear it. It's quite close by.'

Rezzonico smoothed the silk on his lap and smiled:

'As Cardinal Nicolini was saying to me only this morning,' he said, 'your sense of humour, Your Eminence, is a blessing to all of us. He said that it was something that the Sacred College badly needs.'

'That was kind of him.'

'He is a great admirer of yours and, as he went on to say, if he had seen things written about himself such as they are writing about you in the newspapers he would have retired to a monastery for shame for the rest of his days.'

There was a long silence between the two men. At length Di Pino said quietly, 'Would Your Eminence care to see this morning's journal?'

'Perhaps I'd better,' said Capuano. He patted the pockets of his soutane, and then he apologized, 'I am very sorry, but I have forgotten to bring my reading glasses.'

Di Pino nodded. 'With Your Eminence's permission, I shall read you from this morning's *Il Lavoratore*. It is a Communist journal, as you know, but it is the first to come out into the open. If I may, I shall read you some extracts.'

'His Eminence,' said Rezzonico, 'would prefer that you began at the very beginning.'

'Quite so, Your Eminence,' said Di Pino, and obeyed.

Di Pino read in the soft tones he had learned in the Pontifical Academy for reciting Latin. The young journalist would have been well pleased. His opening paragraphs lost nothing through being read as though they were a page in Tacitus.

Rezzonico played with his ring. He watched Capuano's face. Soon he drew through his nostrils a deep breath of satisfaction. Capuano's saintly pallor had gone. He was blushing. Monsignor Di Pino came to an end of the news item.

'Eminence,' he said, 'there is also a leading article.'

'Read it, monsignor,' said Capuano, in a voice that was barely above a whisper. Monsignor Di Pino obeyed. He had got half way through it when Capuano got suddenly to his feet.

'Stop,' he said. He crossed quickly to Di Pino and demanded to be given the paper. Di Pino, who had risen to his feet, handed him the journal with a little bow. Capuano held it away from himself to the full extent of his arm and screwed up his eyes in an endeavour to read it. The paper trembled.

'Who wrote it?' he asked. 'Who wrote it?'

'The editor, I think,' said Rezzonico. 'At least, I feel sure he gave it the final touches. I detect his style. In spite of his politics, he is a highly educated man.'

'The man is a fool, a rogue, and a liar,' said Capuano, and the paper shook more violently in his hand.

'He is quite unspeakable,' replied Rezzonico. 'The only thing that can be said in his favour is the picture he chose of you – that large one in the middle of the front page is really quite flattering. In the ones he prints of me, I always have my mouth wide open and my eyes bolting out of my head as though I am thundering a sentence of excommunication, which, of course, is the impression he wishes to achieve. Give His Eminence the magnifying-glass, Di Pino,' said Rezzonico, 'so that His Eminence can see for himself.'

Capuano spread the paper on the desk and, using the magnifying-glass, studied the photograph of himself with a thurible in his hand, in the act of blessing some glass apparatus. He went on to read a paragraph or two of the leading article. Then he thumped the glass on the paper till Rezzonico feared that it would break.

'The man is a liar,' he said. 'They explained to me quite clearly what the factory was producing.'

'The laboratory,' corrected Rezzonico.

'It was an acid,' said Capuano, ignoring him. 'It was something that you injected into trees and plants to make them grow faster. I remember they showed me some pictures of fruit. Quite enormous fruit they were. I was very impressed. They told me the name of the stuff. It was an acid, a something-or-other acid,' said Capuano, banging the table once more with the magnifying-glass.

'It was,' said Rezzonico, smoothing his silk skirt, which fell over his knee, 'an aphrodisiac.'

'Then you believe this ... this catch-penny trash,' said Capuano. He was unable to prevent his voice from trembling. 'I have always avoided reading cheap newspapers myself for the good reason that one ends by taking them seriously.'

'I,' said Rezzonico, 'read at least six newspapers every day of my life, and I can assure Your Eminence that you are right. They are most certainly full of trash.'

Capuano sat once more on the couch. The flush had drained from his face. He looked at the tall, impassive man beside him.

'Then you agree that this is all a concoction? It is probably the beginning of a new campaign against the Vatican.'

'I think,' said Rezzonico, nodding slowly, 'that, once again, Your Eminence is right. The figs would suggest a campaign. Of ridicule, I should imagine. It is a powerful weapon against us.'

'Ah!' said Capuano. 'The figs.'

'We each got a basket, by messenger, this morning. You got yours?' he asked, solicitously.

'Yes.'

'I don't know who sent them. Do you? No. I see you don't. A Roman, I think, must have been responsible. It is,' said

Rezzonico, with a disdainful Northerner's sniff for the vulgarity of the south, 'a typically coarse Roman joke.'

'I have seen them making horns with their fingers behind their backs when I have passed in a car.' Capuano agreed. He drew a deep breath. 'Well, at least I am glad I have not made a complete fool of myself. None of us can help what the newspapers write about us. But at least the acid or whatever the wretched thing was – at least that's all right.'

'Ah!' said Rezzonico, smoothing his lap for a second time. 'Unfortunately, Your Eminence, it isn't. As I was about to tell Your Eminence when you, quite rightly, lost your temper with that abominable journal, last night we received by express delivery a letter from this English Vassily ... Veezley ... how is it pronounced Di Pino?'

Di Pino told him. Rezzonico repeated it several times, carefully. Capuano held his breath.

'A letter,' Rezzonico resumed, 'from this Dr Wesley. It said that, in the course of his experiments, a moral problem had arisen of great importance to those in the Church and those without. He respectfully requested an urgent interview with someone in the Holy Office. It is easy to put two and two together. I mean,' said Rezzonico, impressively, 'to see Dr Veezley myself.' He looked round his long nose at Capuano. 'Yes,' he said, 'an aphrodisiac, I am very much afraid. Di Pino,' he went on, cheerfully, 'there is somebody tapping at the door. I think they must have brought the coffee.'

*

Maria had watched the Cardinal's car from her window until it was out of sight. Then she made up her mind to find out what had happened. Like the Cardinal, Maria did not read the newspapers, nor did she listen to the radio. She had long ago decided that she could not find time for such things because she was too busy looking after the Cardinal's affairs.

It was true that he had few wants, but he had innumerable relatives. When the red hat had come (or so it seemed to Maria) these had unanimously decided that their troubles were over in this world, and probably in the next, too. These relatives were Maria's special care and she spent long hours worrying over them, separating the sheep from the goats, so as to be ready after supper when the Cardinal answered his letters.

But although she did not read the newspapers, she had her means of finding out what she wanted to know. It cost her an effort. It meant going through the Gate of St Anne, out into the world. Inside the gate, she was Cardinal Capuano's Maria, and the guards said 'Good morning' and 'Good evening'. Outside the gate, as she well knew, she was an ugly old woman with grey hair who talked to herself in the street. Inside the gate, she was the handmaiden they spoke about in the Bible : outside, she was a woman who had wasted her life looking after a priest. The men pitied her, or laughed at her : the women showed her their children.

Still, that morning she put on her hat, and went. As she passed through the Gate of St Anne, the Swiss Guard put a finger to his bonnet, as he always did. Then the Swiss Guard winked, which was a thing that he had never done before. She was well among the traffic and the crowds outside before she got over her indignation. She wondered if there was something exceptionally strange or comic about her appearance. She straightened her hat and tucked away her grey hairs. She pulled down her dress so that it was less wrinkled. She determined to be especially careful that morning in what she did. Her family had always prophesied that she would end up as being a crazy old woman. Perhaps that was what was happening.

'Perhaps it is, Ma,' said a passing errand-boy, 'and at your time of life, too. Shame on you.'

Maria walked on, pressing her lips so tightly together to prevent herself talking aloud that they went white.

She walked past the bright shop windows and gleaming motor-cars, feeling shabby and old in the Roman sunlight. She crossed the road, forgetting the traffic lights, and a policeman in white blew his whistle at her. He pointed at the lights, shook his head and wagged his finger comically at her. When she took no notice of his warning, and carried on across the road, she saw him shrug his shoulders and turn away. She remembered that, once before, when crossing this same road she had nearly been run down. Reaching the pavement, she had heard someone say, 'Drunkards and old women always get across the road in safety.' Walking still more quickly, she wondered if she were going to cry. It wouldn't matter. They would think she was a widow; or perhaps a mother bereaved of her child.

But she did not cry. Instead, she lost her temper with herself. 'Here you are,' she said, aloud, 'being sorry for yourself and the Cardinal's in trouble. Who's going to help him if you don't, I'd like to know?'

A man walking in front of her, surprised by her voice, turned round and said, 'Madam?' He saw the expression on her face, touched his hat respectfully and walked off. To keep her mind on her business, Maria took her rosary from her black handbag and, holding it in one hand, told the beads with a cracked thumbnail. By the time she had reached the place she was making for she was herself again.

It was a café on the corner of the street. Tables and chairs were strung out along two side-walks : inside there was a bar and a place for eating. As Maria approached, a plump, elderly waiter threw wide his arms in welcome, and shuffled out to meet her. He guided her to a table and sat her down in a chair. When she was about to give her order, he archly put his fingers to his lips and disappeared into the bar. A little later he came out bearing a long glass of green syrup, the one luxury that Maria allowed herself. 'With the compliments of the management,' he said, 'to Sister Maria.'

She had no right to the title, but it pleased her. She smiled for the first time since she had left the Gate of St Anne.

'Well, Enzo, and what is the news this morning?'

A long time ago someone had said to Maria, 'Well, so now your Capuano's a bishop, and from now on he'll never miss a meal and never hear the truth.' It was a saying that was common enough among the faithful, but to Maria it pointed out a new duty. It was her job to listen to gossip. She had done so to Capuano's great advantage. But when he got to the Vatican, she soon found that the gossip there was of no use to her. She heard a great deal about the other prelates, but nothing whatever about her own master. She had assumed that it was the code of the place and looked elsewhere for her information. She found it in the Borgo.

The Borgo is that part of the City of Rome which lies underneath the walls of the Vatican, and it has for centuries known a great deal about what goes on inside them. It prides itself on looking with an amused, cynical, and civilian eye on the doings of priests, for it is here that the civilians who work in the Vatican come to relax and gossip in the long summer evenings. They go, above all, to the café on the corner where Maria now sat sipping her glass of green syrup.

Enzo had always been very willing to tell Maria all that he had heard. But this morning he made a gesture of extreme astonishment.

'You ask *me*, Sister Maria, for the news,' he said. 'What can I, a poor little man with flat feet, who never leaves this café, except to go home to bed, tell *you*, Sister Maria? You, who took the Cardinal's coffee to him this very morning. What did he say when he saw the newspapers?'

Enzo was talking very loudly in his excitement. People at

the other tables turned and, smiling, looked at her. Men were crowding in the doorway of the bar. One of them said: 'Yes, what did he say?' and laughed loudly.

'His Eminence hasn't seen the newspapers,' said Maria.

Enzo said, 'Have you?'

Maria replied, 'No.'

'She doesn't know. She hasn't heard,' said Enzo, delightedly, to the world at large. 'Then I, Enzo, shall tell you. His Eminence's nephew has gone into the patent medicine business,' he said. There was loud laughter from everybody in the café.

'What sort of medicine?' said Maria.

'What sort, what sort?' Enzo crowed. 'This sort, Sister Maria. Just one drop and even I, poor Enzo with the flat feet and a wife and ten children, will be able to make love like a sailor home from a cruise. Forgive me for saying such things to a lady like yourself. But what harm can there be? Your reverend master, His Eminence himself, has given it his blessing, holy water and all.'

He seized a glass of water and a fork and, intoning through his nose, sprinkled the men in the doorway, to their uproarious delight. When they had stopped laughing, Maria said, 'What is this nephew's name?'

One of the men in the doorway pulled a newspaper from his pocket and consulted it.

'His name's Pozzo. *Pozzo's Pink Potency Potion*,' he said, '*as approved by the clergy*.'

The laughter, now, was unbounded. Maria stared down at the green liquid in her glass. Pozzo was the Cardinal's favourite relative, and hers, too.

*

Rezzonico asked Di Pino to be so good as to read Harry's letter aloud to His Eminence. Capuano listened until the end.

139

'Thank you,' he said, 'I agree. There can be no doubt.' There was silence for a while in the room. Then Capuano said, with great simplicity:

'I have always known I was something of a fool. But I did not think I would ever be so foolish as to cause scandal to the Holy Church. Yet that is just what I have done.'

'This Pozzo,' said Rezzonico. 'Your nephew . . .'

'Oh,' said Capuano, quickly. 'It's not his fault.'

'Then you trust him?'

'Of course. He is my favourite nephew.'

'Ah!' said Rezzonico, 'but the history of the Church suggests that ecclesiastics should be particularly careful of favourite nephews.'

'Does it?' Capuano stirred sugar into his now cold coffee, absently. 'I have never read much of it. I sometimes think that the history of the Church should be left to those who do not wish her particularly well.'

'That is a profound thought, Your Eminence,' said Rezzonico. 'But,' he added with a touch of bullying in his tone, 'I was just wanting to make sure that we won't have that newspaper running articles for the next month about nepotism in the Vatican. Not wishing the Church at all well, they know a good deal of its history.'

'Well,' said Capuano, mildly, 'he *is* my nephew. And I *am* fond of him. I did pay for his education. And as a matter of fact I know he made great play with my name when he went into politics. Have you no relatives, Rezzonico?'

'Several,' said Rezzonico, sharply. 'But they are still the small shopkeepers and clerks that they were when – when I took holy orders. Not one of them is an Under-Secretary of State.'

'Andrea isn't a very grand Under-Secretary. I think they only put him in to balance a Liberal they were forced to take. The nephew of a cardinal seemed a suitable choice, so Andrea got the job.' Capuano broke off. 'There again, you see.

Nepotism. Nepotism of the first water.' He drank his cold coffee. 'But all this business isn't Pozzo's fault. He's a good fellow. You'd like him if you met him. He has something of Your Eminence's drive and energy. But,' said Capuano, pausing, 'he has no guile. No guile at all.'

Di Pino stole a glance at Rezzonico to see how his master had taken this gentlest of thrusts. Rezzonico's large nose was a fraction higher in the air.

'No,' Capuano went on. 'It must be the fault of this Englishman. He has made some mistake. It is curious to think of an Englishman making a blunder. It is more the sort of thing we Italians expect to find ourselves doing. Yes, it is the Englishman's fault. But that doesn't excuse me in the least. But I know what I shall do.'

'It is most important,' said Rezzonico, 'that we do nothing precipitately.'

'It is most important that you do nothing precipitately,' said Capuano. 'But for me the quicker the better. I shall take Cardinal Nicolini's hint. I shall retire to a monastery. He is quite right. It is the proper place for a prelate in disgrace. I shall make a full confession of my stupidity and my folly. I shall preach a sermon, I think. Yes, a sermon . . .' he said, his gaze wandering abstractedly to the window. 'Poor Maria,' he whispered. 'It will break her heart.'

'Your Eminence,' said Rezzonico, firmly. 'Will you please listen to me for a few moments?'

'Certainly, Rezzonico. Certainly.'

'Your Eminence's withdrawal to a monastery would be an act of deep Christian humility and personal reparation. I greatly respect your decision. It does you great honour. Unfortunately, it does nothing whatever to solve the problem you have set the Church. This liquid . . . this acid . . . this fertilizer . . . whatever it is, is not only an evil thing. It is also a very good thing. It is not only the work of the Devil. It is the work of Divine Providence.'

He paused to see the effect of his words. Capuano was most suitably bewildered. Rezzonico went on :

'You have overlooked, if I may venture to say so, the fact that this thing produces fruit of an astonishing size. It will be a blessing to our farmers. It will bring prosperity to this impoverished land of ours . . .'

'That is exactly what they told me . . .' Capuano interjected.

'. . . it will be like manna from heaven to countless Italian families,' Rezzonico continued, 'whose only other hope of a decent human existence would be to emigrate to one of the few distant countries that will still let them in. And this, Your Eminence, is the thing you would have the Church condemn out of hand because it is also a . . . a . . . stimulant. Your sermon will undoubtedly be a most moving one. But within twenty-four hours of its delivery, we shall have the whole country about our ears. We shall be accused of snatching the bread from the mouths of little children. We shall be accused of obstructing the progress of science. We shall be accused of being bigoted priests with an unhealthy interest in sex. I trust my plain speaking does not offend Your Eminence?'

'No . . . no . . . I am not offended,' said Capuano. 'I confess it was something I had not thought of. And yet, if it is the work of the Devil – and Your Eminence has admitted that it is – then surely we must fight it, whatever the world will say of us.'

'In a long life of service to the Church,' Rezzonico answered, 'I have come to the conclusion that one of the functions of the Devil is to make priests use their brains. Consider for a moment, Your Eminence. You were born, I believe, in the South.'

'I was born in Puglia,' said Capuano, nodding.

'Then you have seen for yourself the poverty and misery there. And as a priest you have seen the sins to which poverty gives rise. I, too, for a time, have worked there. Incest, murder, and horrors I shall not name because they are as familiar to me as they are, I am sure, to you.'

'It is true,' said Capuano. 'For three years I refused a bishopric because I thought my duty lay among those poor ...' He did not finish his sentence, but tears stood in his eyes.

'And yet this thing the Englishman has brought here may bring these people, who have suffered the worst degradations that can be inflicted upon a human being, into the light – into the cleanliness, the hope, the moral resolution of a man who is sure of two meals a day and food enough for his family to see his children grow straight-limbed. Does not that thought suggest to you that we should move with all caution in this matter? The thing is dangerous. Yes. But is the danger in it any more than the danger which our mother Eve brought into the world when she ate the fruit of the forbidden tree? Is it not the same danger that the Church has fought since its foundation, but fought by teaching men to restrain themselves, to control their lusts, and to use their passions, however strong they may be, to ends that are pleasing in the sight of God?'

'But, Eminence,' said Capuano, speaking slowly and hesitantly, 'it was not only for eating the fruit of *that* tree that our first parents were driven out of Eden.'

'I have always thought it was,' said Rezzonico, bringing his great nose round to face Capuano.

'Then I must be wrong,' said Capuano. 'But surely there was another tree.'

Capuano raised his mild eyes to meet those of Rezzonico.

Then he quoted in the soft, sibilant Latin that priests speak in the South, the verses that in English are, '"The Lord God said, Behold, the man is become as one of us, to know good and evil: and now, lest he put forth his hand

143

and take also of the tree of life,"' Capuano waited a moment, and then finished, ' "and eat, and live for ever. Therefore the Lord God sent him forth from the garden of Eden." Rezzonico,' he said, 'I am afraid of this Englishman and the things he is doing. Were there, perhaps, two temptations in the Garden? And is it now the time for the second?'

He spread his hands wide. 'I don't know. I feel, with Your Eminence's permission, I would like to go and give the Devil his due, and use my brains, as you suggest. I must have time to think a little . . .'

'By all means,' said Rezzonico, rising.

'. . . before I go into the monastery,' said Capuano, rising as well. 'Because that I am quite determined to do.'

They walked together to the door. Monsignors ran down the corridor as the door opened. They formed a cardinal's guard of honour and accompanied the two Princes of the Church to the point where protocol allowed them to take leave of each other.

*

Rezzonico returned to his room, Di Pino following him. His Eminence's expression was composed and smiling until they had shut the door, but once in the room he made no attempt to hide his ill-humour. He strode up and down for a few moments, a magnificent and awesome figure in his scarlet robes. Then he regained control of himself. He stopped. He turned to Di Pino.

'Well,' he said, 'at least His Eminence has one characteristic of a saint.'

'What is that, Eminence?' Di Pino inquired, respectfully.

'Pig-headedness,' Rezzonico snapped. 'And now he will go off to his monastery and leave all the thinking for me to do.'

He sat at his desk. He ran his hands over his face and massaged his eyes. He sighed.

'Well, then, let's begin. Where is this wretched Englishman?'

'In the South, Eminence,' said Di Pino, and named the village.

'And how are we going to get into touch with him there without every newspaper in the land knowing it?' asked Rezzonico. 'If we telegraph, the clerk will sell the message. If we write, they'll steal the letter and photograph it.'

'We could telephone the bishop, Eminence.'

Rezzonico thought for a moment.

'Good. Please be so good as to do that. And scare the daylights out of him so that he doesn't go gossiping with his canons.'

Di Pino bowed and saying, 'With your leave, Eminence,' he lifted the telephone. He spoke to the operator in the calm level tones prescribed for making a call in the Vatican.

In the Ministry of Agriculture, however, at much the same moment, the telephone operator's heart was in his throat. He had never heard such barking since the days of Fascism. Terrified by Pozzo's voice, he muddled the calls. When finally he managed to connect Pozzo with an army general, he heard Pozzo use the word 'emergency' and, convinced that war had broken out, he burst into hysterical tears.

But Pozzo, enormously enjoying himself, was only demanding that Harry's fig tree be put under a heavy armed guard with instructions to shoot any marauders on sight.

*

That morning Joe woke in his four-poster bed after a dreamless night. He lay in bed for a while listening to the noise of the sea below his villa. Then it struck him that he had had no dreams. He looked at his bedclothes. They were neat

145

and orderly. He got out of bed. He looked in a mirror. He clapped his hands like a happy child. He returned to his bed and rang the bell for Minu. When his butler came into the room, he found his master sitting up in bed and looking at him with a most curious expression.

'Good morning, *signor*,' said the butler.

'Good morning, Minu.'

Minu went to the window to throw it open, as he always did. 'It'll be cooler today, *signor*,' he said. 'The north wind's...'

'Never mind the weather,' said Joe. 'How do I look?'

Minu turned back towards the bed. 'Look, *signor*?'

'Yes. Do I look as well as I did yesterday?'

'Certainly, sir.'

'Minu, look again. Look closely.'

Minu peered.

'No, *signor*. I am sorry to say you do not.'

'I don't glow with health, eh?'

'No, *signor*.'

'My eyes don't sparkle, eh?'

'No, *signor*. Are you feeling unwell, *signor*?'

'I feel,' said Joe, solemnly, 'as though I have recovered from a long and dangerous illness.'

'That's strange, *signor*,' said Minu. 'I thought you'd been looking particularly well these last few days.'

'Yes,' said Joe, even more solemnly. 'But that, I think, is over. Thank God,' he added, fervently.

Back in the kitchen, the cook's wife asked:

'And how's the old basket this morning?'

'Much as usual. Kept asking me to look at him. "Look at me, Minu," he said. I ask you. At this hour in the morning, before I've had my third cup of coffee. So I stared at his ugly mug and I said, "*Signor*, you look like something that the cat brought in."'

'You did?' said the cook's wife, contemptuously clattering the dishes on Joe's breakfast tray.

'One day I will, so help me,' said Minu.

'Not while you play the horses, you won't,' said the cook's wife. 'What did he want you to look at him for?'

'I dunno. He thinks he's feeling sick, or something. You don't think I listen to the old fool's drivel, do you? As a matter of fact,' Minu added, thoughtfully, 'he didn't look as well as he did. If you ask me, the Countess has had enough of him. And no wonder. A fine-looking woman falling for an old goat like him. Well,' he said, and sighed heavily, 'I suppose it's his money she was after.'

'I'm glad to hear it,' said the cook's wife. 'We don't want a woman in the house.'

'No,' Minu agreed. 'One's enough, God knows.' With that, he opened a racing newspaper and began making crosses with a pencil.

*

Joe ate breakfast. He bathed, shaved, dressed, and then, to the sound of an imaginary orchestra, he danced in a stately, eighteenth-century fashion round and round the drawing-room. There was no doubt of it. The thing had passed.

He stopped dancing and ran his eye lovingly over the furniture and the bric-à-brac in the room. For days he had barely known where he was, so great had been the tumult in his flesh and in his spirit.

'Now it's gone,' he said, aloud, 'it's like coming home after staying a long, long time in someone else's house.'

He walked out upon the terrace.

'But then, of course,' he said to himself, 'it was someone else in my house, wasn't it?'

Then he heard a boy whistling. The boy was whistling through his teeth. He was whistling through his teeth and he was whistling an American popular tune.

147

All these things were strange. Boys along the coast rarely whistled and never through their teeth. They sang, but rarely in tune: and they sang only Neapolitan songs.

The whistling came from above Joe's house. He moved from under a vine and looked up.

The whistling boy was Harry.

Harry saw him and waved. He put his hands to his mouth and shouted:

'Joe! How are you feeling?'

'Wonderful,' shouted Joe. 'It's gone.'

'Me too,' shouted Harry. 'I haven't felt like this since I was a boy. I was coming down to see you.'

'No,' shouted Joe. 'I'll come up to you. I feel like some exercise.'

*

They met half-way.

'When did it happen to you?' Harry asked.

'I noticed it first when I woke up this morning.' said Joe. 'And you?'

'I didn't get much sleep last night. No, it wasn't dreams. I was out on the terrace. Do you know what I was doing? I was cutting every damned fig off that tree and taking them down to the sea in a basket and dumping them in the water. It took me until three o'clock, but I was determined to get the thing done. Then I lay on the bed to rest before undressing and having a shower. I must have fallen asleep. I woke up about seven and ... well,' said Harry. He grinned and once more began whistling through his teeth like a street urchin.

Suddenly he stopped.

'Look,' he said. 'There's a woman coming up the path.'

'She's the milk-maid.'

'She's pretty,' said Harry.

'Eh?' said Joe.

'She's got a well-developed bust,' said Harry.

'Harry! For heaven's sake,' said Joe, in dismay.

'She's got good hips on her,' went on Harry, remorselessly. 'In fact, she's a dish.'

'Harry!' said Joe, in a wail.

'I propose,' said Harry, 'that we make a scientific experiment. We will both go up to this dish. We will both carry on a light and flippant conversation with her. We will both gaze, with all due deliberation, at her bosom and her other charms. We will both observe the results.'

'No, Harry,' said Joe. 'It's too much of a risk.'

'It's the only way of being sure,' said Harry, firmly.

'But supposing the whole thing starts up again?'

'Then we will be martyrs to science. Courage, Joe. Think of the man who discovered chloroform and tried it on himself. Think of the men who injected themselves with serums ...'

'They use rats,' said Joe, obstinately.

'Unfortunately in this instance there is no way that a rat can be employed. Besides, you object to experiments on animals. You told me so. Here she comes now. Forward, Joe, into the Unknown. Forward on Man's deathless quest for knowledge. Say something to her.'

'What?' said Joe, desperately.

'Where are you going to, my pretty maid?' Harry suggested. But the girl saved Joe the trouble by flashing him a wide smile and saying, '*Buon giorno, signori. Che bella giornata!*'

'*Buon giorno*,' Joe answered, in a quavering voice. Seeing the two foreigners looking at her, the girl advanced boldly upon them. Joe fell back a pace, but he felt Harry's hand in the small of his back.

'Four minutes by my watch,' Harry whispered to Joe. 'That should be enough to tell.' He smiled at the girl, who flashed her eyes at him, having already flashed her teeth several times.

'Good morning. It is indeed a beautiful day,' said Harry,

in careful and slow Italian. 'I was saying to my friend that you are so pretty you should be on the films.'

Since this was exactly what foreigners said to country girls in the movie-magazines which she devoured each week, she knew just how to keep the conversation going. She was, in fact, in complete command of herself for she had rehearsed just such a meeting in her mind for years. She heaved her bosom. She lowered her eyelids. She said she was just a country girl, but that life was so narrow that sometimes she felt suffocated. She stretched her neck: she slightly parted her lips: she suffocated. She said she always wanted to be an actress and repeated the sentiment with every readily movable part of her body.

Her remarks were lost on Harry and Joe. Her words were those of the magazines, but her dialect was that of the peasants, who, in the South, are incomprehensible a mile away from their birthplaces. But Harry observed her closely, nodding when he thought fit, and Joe, curiosity overcoming his fears, did the same.

The girl was so convinced that she was making an overwhelming impression that she was taken aback when one of the two foreigners looked at his watch and said something in English, at which both men bid her a sharp good-bye. They strode off side by side down the road.

'Feel anything?' asked Harry.

'Nothing at all,' said Joe.

'Nor me,' said Harry. He whistled a marching tune, and the two men fell into step.

'Learned that tune in the Scouts,' said Harry. 'Used to play a bugle. They were happy days.'

They walked a little further in silence.

'Girls,' said Harry, contemptuously. 'Girls are soppy.'

'Complete *wets*,' agreed Joe. 'I can't think what all the fuss is about.'

'Especially that one,' said Harry. 'Wriggling like an eel.'

'Awful,' agreed Joe.

'Tell you what,' said Harry, as they marched along. 'Dare you to shout "Milk-ho!" at her.'

'And I double-dare you,' said Joe.

The milk-maid, watching the two men, was puzzled to hear the young one shout a word in English followed by a long yodelling sound. She raised her hand in reply, in case it should have been meant for her.

'Look out!' said Harry. 'She's heard us! Run!'

The milk-maid saw the two men, now, she presumed, entirely out of their senses, scamper wildly down the road together. She dropped her hand and resumed her walk, frowning and sucking her teeth in great perplexity.

As Harry ran, he saw the path that led down to the rocks from which Joe bathed. He saw some huts and a springboard.

'Joe!' he said, still running.

'Yes?' panted Joe.

Harry pointed down to the rocks.

'Last-one-in's-a-silly-fool!' he shouted, and bounded down the path.

*

Joe was splashing in the water, and Harry was doing vertical jumps off the diving-board, holding his nose like a small boy, when Isabella arrived to do her usual morning's work on Joe's accounts.

She heard them shouting. She went to the terrace. They saw her leaning over the parapet and shouted their 'good mornings'.

'Harry,' she called down, 'you're in the newspaper. Have you seen it yet?'

'No.'

'I'll leave it here on the seat for you to read.'

'I'll be up directly,' shouted Harry.

Isabella gazed at both of them with a deeply thoughtful

expression, as they climbed out of the water. Then she went inside the house.

Joe was dressed first and came up to the terrace. He saw the newspaper lying on the seat, but then catching Isabella's eye through the window, he went straight in to her.

'What have they written about Harry, Isabella?' Joe asked.

She had got up from her desk when he came in. She looked at him squarely.

'They have written, Joe, about Harry's figs,' she said, with deliberation.

'Good Lord. How much?'

'All that was necessary to make things quite clear.'

'But how could they have found out, Isabella?'

'It seems that Harry confessed everything in a moment of depression to some parish priest in Calabria.'

Joe was shocked.

'What a thing to do! He blabs everything to a complete stranger, while he absolutely forbade me to utter a word to . . .' Joe stopped in confusion.

'To me, Joe?' said Isabella.

Joe blushed deeply.

'I'm very sorry,' he said. 'Very, very sorry.'

'So it wasn't just Harry who ate . . . No,' said Isabella. 'I suppose you both made a great banquet off them. I can see you both.'

'It was all rather hole-in-the-corner,' said Joe, in a small voice. 'Minu bribed Harry's girl to steal one.'

'And you ate it?'

Joe, not trusting himself to speak, nodded.

Isabella looked away from him. She said nothing at all. Then Joe said:

'Isabella, I did want to tell you, you remember. I felt – it's impossible to tell you how ashamed I felt. And I do still.'

She looked back at him.

'There's no need to be sorry, Joe,' she said. 'In 1569, one of the della Quercias of the Padua branch of our family ...' She stopped abruptly. She turned on her heel. She walked to the desk, and riffled through some letters. She opened the book in which the cook kept his accounts.

'There is something I must tell you about your cook, Joe,' she said, briskly. But Joe said:

'*What* happened in 1569, Isabella?'

Isabella bent her head over the cook's book.

'It doesn't matter, Joe,' she said. 'I was only making it up.'

*

Harry came into the room, the paper in his hand. He looked alarmed.

'Isabella,' he said. 'The Italian's too difficult for me, but from what I can read of it this doesn't look good. I can see my name, and the picture of the Cardinal, but what worries me most is seeing Don Ugo's name. Will you translate it for me?'

'Willingly, Harry,' said Isabella, taking the paper. 'But I should tell you, as I've just told Joe, that they have the whole story. Your Don Ugo told them.'

'Don Ugo!' exclaimed Harry. 'The rogue! The scoundrel! The traitor! The sneak!! I'll denounce him to his bishop. I'll ...

The other things Harry was going to do to him were lost in a sudden pandemonium of sirens, klaxons, motor engines, and shouts, that broke out over their heads.

All three of them went out on to the terrace. They saw that the noise was coming from the road that led to Harry's house. A platoon of troops was dismounting from a truck while staff cars, police cars, and a radio car ran hither and thither, sounding their horns. Army Headquarters had responded with alacrity and dash to Pozzo's demands: in five minutes Harry's house and the terrace on which the fig

153

tree grew were ringed with armed soldiers, the roads leading to it had been commanded, and vantage points in the surrounding area had been efficiently occupied by armed patrols. An officer, whose epaulettes flashed in the sunlight, could be seen talking to Harry's orphan girl, who appeared, even from a distance, to be hysterical.

Though it could not be observed by Harry, Joe, and Isabella, the consternation among the surrounding farmers was profound. They bolted the doors of their houses and peered through the windows. Their suspicious were confirmed. As they had guessed all along, Harry was an excise agent: and, it would appear, a good one. He had observed their illicit doings, by the light of his lamps, and now here was the reckoning. Some of the farmers, with true Southern passion, prepared to sell their lives dearly: others prepared to sell their friends. Harry's orphan girl, in a torrent of words, told the Captain who was questioning her everything she knew, except Harry's whereabouts, which was the only thing that interested him. She quietened down after five minutes sufficiently to point, still sobbing, down to Joe's house to indicate where her master could be found. The officer thanked her and made his way down the hill.

He had almost arrived at Joe's front door when he heard footsteps and heavy breathing behind him. He turned to find that he was being followed by the Bishop of Maiori in a state of great agitation. Di Pino had obeyed the Cardinal's instructions. One of the functions of the Holy Office is to discipline the clergy: Di Pino had kept the Bishop guessing for ten minutes on the telephone before he told him what he had to do. In those ten minutes, all the Bishop's sins of omission – for these were his only misdemeanours – had gone through his head. What with the sea, the hot climate, and the Bishop's natural indolence, the list had left him a shaken man.

The Bishop and the Captain entered Joe's house together. Church and State delivered their respective messages. Harry was invited to the Holy Office the following day: Harry's house was to be guarded as vital State property, and the tree – this was a little flourish of Pozzo's, with which he was well pleased – the tree was to be considered a top secret. The Captain, saluting politely, asked Harry if he could have the key to the door in the wire fence.

Harry drew himself up. He spoke in his slow, careful Italian, and he spoke clearly.

'Captain,' he said, 'I shall, on no account, give you or anybody else my key, until I have discharged my moral responsibility to my fellow-men. I am now going to Rome. I shall see His Excellency Andrea Pozzo who is my official superior, and I shall visit the Holy Office where I shall, I believe, meet my betters. I hope to return with the right to have that evil tree torn up by the roots and burned,' he said. Then relapsing into English, 'Preferably by the public hangman.'

Journalists, who had by now crept into the hallway through the open front-door, reported Harry as having defied the Army and as having ended his speech with the cry of 'God Save the Queen!'

THERE is no public hangman in Italy, but otherwise Harry had his own way. The tree was dragged up by the roots. The ground was bulldozed and sterilized, and the tree was burned, not in public, but very thoroughly, and in front of solemn witnesses.

Three things helped to bring this about. The first of them was Maria's obstinacy, for without that Cardinal Capuano would never have preached his famous sermon. After he had seen Rezzonico, he had spent the day in retreat and in prayer. He had emerged with the determination that there was nothing for him to do but to retire to a monastery straight away. The rest he would leave to Rezzonico.

He came back to his lodgings in time for his evening meal. Maria had brought it from the canteen in a container which kept it hot. She laid the table. She served the dish of macaroni which was all that the Cardinal was accustomed to eat. He sat at the table, and she watched him silently. When he was nearly finished she said:

'Don Silvio, you know what the figs were for?'

'Yes, Maria. Do you?'

'Yes. It's all over the Borgo.'

'Maria,' said Silvio Capuano, 'I have caused a grave scandal. I am entirely to blame. I think I should tell you now that I have decided to resign from my present position and to retire to some place where I can end my days without causing further harm.'

'That's Rezzonico's idea, isn't it?' said Maria, bitterly.

'No.'

'What are you going to do about all this mess that Andrea's caused?'

'Nothing. I am not competent to do anything.'

'I thought so,' said Maria. 'You're a saint . . .'

'You're not to use that word, Maria,' said the Cardinal.

'But you've got one weakness. They all had, if you ask me.' She waited for Capuano to speak, but he said nothing for a while. At last he looked at her.

'What is it?'

'You're afraid of being laughed at. You always were, ever since you were a parish priest.' She took away his dish and began to pour his coffee. 'It's because it's about men and women going to bed, isn't it? You never have known much about that except what you read in the book. I know, though,' she said, and set the cup in front of him.

'You, Maria?'

'Yes. I had a lover once.'

Capuano looked at her in astonishment.

'A real lover. A fine lad, he was.'

'But you never told me.'

'I confessed it. Not to you. You were worried, and you weren't well. So I went to the Franciscans.'

'What happened, Maria? Did he want to marry you?'

'Yes. But I gave him up.'

'Why?'

'Because I wanted to look after you.'

Neither of them spoke for a while, and then she went on: 'Don Silvio, do you remember how your church was always full of people when you were a parish priest? And even when you were a bishop, too? Do you ever wonder why all these women came to church and gave money and lit candles and said the rosary each evening? It's because they thought you were a good man. It's because they thought you knew something better than the life they led, going to bed with their husband and bearing children and going to bed with him again when he loved them, when he didn't, when he was sober, when he was drunk, when they wanted him and when they thought that they would kill him if he touched them. They told you their sins, but they didn't tell you this. They told me, though. They showed me their babies to make me jealous. And,' she said, 'I was. I was. But then when they'd had their fun, they told me the truth. That's why they've got to have saints. That's why they listened to you. That's why they still listen to you, and hold up their children to see you when you're in a procession. And that's why,' she said, passionately, 'you've got to tell us that we're right. You. Not Rezzonico. You.'

Capuano looked up at her and saw that tears were streaming down her old face: but for all that she stood straight, with her head high, and her mouth set and firm.

'And as for Andrea,' she said, 'he wants a good box on the ears. I know you won't give him one, so I shall give him one for you. That will settle *him*.'

*

The second factor in getting the tree uprooted was Harry's visit to the Holy Office.

It began most successfully. Harry was flattered to see Monsignor Di Pino waiting for him as his taxi drew up at the entrance to the palace. He was relaxed to find, as they went up in the elevator, that Monsignor Di Pino spoke more than serviceable English, and like all the world, when he met Rezzonico in his damask-lined room, he was impressed by the splendour of his robes. He was about to bow and to make at least a pass at kissing the Cardinal's ring, when Rezzonico seized his hand and shook it heartily.

Harry was conducted to the couch. Di Pino drew up a chair and, acting as an interpreter, conveyed to Harry His Eminence's preliminary courtesies. These went on a considerable time and Harry began to wonder how he could bring the conversation to the point where he could state his business. His eyes wandered round the imposing room.

Rezzonico, noting this, judged it time to explode what he always called his petard.

'Well, now, Doctor Wesley,' he said, genially. 'You are a distinguished scientist. Tell me, what does it feel like to find yourself inside the Holy Office? It was we, you know – and in this very building – who condemned Galileo for saying that the earth moved round the sun.'

Rezzonico asked this question whenever he was visited by a scientist, or a Protestant, or a liberal humanist. It had never failed in its effect. His visitors all felt that this was the last topic they expected to be discussed by a cardinal. They left his presence profoundly impressed, as he intended, by his broadmindedness.

Di Pino translated the question to Harry, and as soon as he had done so, he felt sure that this time it was going to misfire.

'Galileo?' said Harry. 'I've always thought that he was a lucky man to have you gentlemen as his judges. He couldn't go in front of a meeting of present-day physicists and get away with a thing like that. Not nowadays. After all, the general concensus of expert opinion was that the sun went round the earth. Here was this man saying, "Oh, no, it's quite the other way about." But there hadn't been any teamwork done on it; it hadn't been in the air; it hadn't been kicked around the learned societies. Nowadays, he'd have been treated as a madman, a charlatan, or as a danger to professional standards. Everybody believes that the world of science hangs round its lab benches waiting for a genius. We don't. We like to know which way the cat's going to jump. Anybody who can make it jump a bit further than was expected gets a pat on the back. But woe betide anybody who makes it jump in the opposite direction. If Galileo had been judged by *us* he would probably have lost his job and starved; whereas you gentlemen only confined him to his apartment, I believe. Most reasonable. Most far-sighted. You gentlemen were the first people to see that scientists are, by and large, *up to no good*,' said Harry, emphasizing his words with an uplifted forefinger. 'I take off my hat to you. That's why I'm here today.'

Rezzonico, when, at last, Harry paused to let him say something, was much less genial. He raised his large nose a trifle and said:

'But that, Doctor Wesley, is a very common misconception of the attitude of the Church, particularly among people who are fond of talking about her without knowing very much about the subject. We do not, by any means, think that scientists are immoral. They may – they very often do – act from the highest motives.'

'They *begin* that way,' said Harry. 'I began by wanting to save humanity. In the end the only part of humanity that was of any real concern to me is sitting in this chair and listening to Your Eminence.'

Rezzonico raised his hand. 'Dear me, no,' he said, smiling bleakly. 'It is I who have the honour of listening and a great privilege I am finding it. But it still remains,' he said, with a trace of sharpness, 'that we do not blame the scientists. However, we are sometimes forced to point out that the discoveries they make are often put to uses which are in defiance of the laws of God. This we condemn and condemn again.'

'Eminence,' said Harry. 'If I had a gun and I shot it out of the window and it killed someone, would you condemn me?'

'It would depend,' said the Cardinal. He fiddled with his ring a moment. 'It might be for self-defence. In that case, I would prefer you did not shoot it out of *my* window,' said the Cardinal, but Harry brushed his pleasantry aside.

'Suppose I said I fired it to test a hypothesis I had about the trajectory of bullets.'

Since the Cardinal did not reply immediately, Harry was

about to explain further when Rezzonico said, with open irritation to Di Pino, in Italian:

'Please make clear that I quite see what he is driving at. I am not a complete fool.'

'His Eminence,' said Di Pino, 'fully understands your point. You are saying that the scientist . . .'

'I'm saying that he refuses to consider the results of what he is doing and just does it claiming heaven knows what high motives. And I'm saying that *that* is immoral. If it isn't, I don't know what immorality is.'

'You speak with deep sincerity,' said Rezzonico. 'With most moving sincerity.' He paused. 'Surely, my son, what you are saying is that you feel that *you* have done wrong.'

'It is. And I have done wrong.'

'Your humility does you credit,' said Rezzonico.

'Begging your pardon,' said Harry, 'but I don't know that I do feel humble. I feel angry. With myself maybe. But with my colleagues and fellow-workers, too. That's why I've come here. I want to ask you to tell us all – everybody who'll listen to you – and that will be hundreds of millions – that we stand in great danger. We stand in danger of having our lives twisted, our souls and our bodies destroyed, by men who boast that they are above right and wrong. And I think this scandalous thing that I have hit upon would make a fine jumping-off point. Particularly,' Harry finished, 'since I will be there to back up every word you say.'

'I understand you are not a member of our Church,' said Rezzonico.

'No.'

'Nevertheless,' said Rezzonico, 'heaven, we are assured, may be taken by storm. But you were speaking of your experiments. Would you, perhaps, tell me more about them?'

Harry obliged. It was a great mistake. For at one point in his explanation he said:

'Pozzo was in a hurry. Funds were running out. So I doubled the dose.'

Rezzonico brought his great nose to bear full on Harry.

'But that may have caused the change in the effects of your fertilizer. Or am I being very stupid?'

'It might,' said Harry. 'But that just supports my point. I agreed to use it, without the slightest thought of the possible consequences.'

'Pozzo, you say, asked for it.'

'Yes.'

Rezzonico smoothed the silk on his lap. Harry proceeded with his explanation, but he was soon conscious that he was losing his audience. Di Pino's translation became slower and clumsier. The Cardinal fiddled with his ring. When Rezzonico assured him that he appreciated his zeal, but that the Church must act with all due caution, he knew he was being dismissed. He left the Holy Office a deeply disappointed man.

'A most interesting chat,' said Rezzonico, smiling, to Di Pino, when Harry had gone. 'The Church has been thoroughly instructed in her duties and I personally have been given my battle orders.'

'Your Eminence was very forbearing with the young man,' said Di Pino.

'If I hadn't been,' said Rezzonico, 'he would never have let slip that thing about Pozzo.'

'Pozzo,' His Eminence repeated, and looked a very satisfied man.

*

The third factor in uprooting the tree was Isabella.

Harry returned to the South to find his house uninhabitable. His orphan girl had fled, and no one else would work for him. Besides, the place was surrounded day and night by photographers and journalists.

So he stayed in Joe's blue guest-room. The following

163

evening Isabella came to dinner. Afterwards they sat on a small cramped terrace which was the only place where they could be sure they would not be photographed.

'I wouldn't mind the publicity,' said Harry, 'if only I could have persuaded Rezzonico to do something. It would have been just the thing. But now it's wasted. The papers are just making things up. And they get sillier every day – even sillier than the one that said I bellowed "God Save the Queen" in that officer's face. It's no use. I can't do anything. I'm a foreigner among a strange people and the only thing they know about me is that I've seduced one of their women. What I want,' he said, 'is some way of talking to them. Some way of getting my point across.'

'This is one of the few times,' said Joe, sympathetically, 'when I wish my family were here. They are so good at running campaigns of this sort. They control one third of the advertising in America.'

'*Your* family,' said Isabella. 'What about mine? We spend more money in newspapers, television, billboards, than ...' She stopped. 'Billboards,' she said. Then, writing the words with her forefinger in the air. 'I can see them – PROTECT YOUR FAMILY.' It was at that moment that Harry's campaign was born.

With true Quercia dash, Isabella caught the night train to her family headquarters in Milan. Neither the ice-cream side nor the mineral water side took much persuading. The slogan touched the chords of the Italian heart, it was clean and healthy, like their ice-cream and soft drinks. Lastly, they had not had a new promotional idea for a year.

In ten days the whole country was roused. The Italian people learned, with horror, that an attack had been made on the sanctity of family life by a foul drug manufactured under Government auspices. They learned that its inventor, an Englishman, had been overcome with justifiable remorse and was fully supporting the campaign. Mothers, wives, and sisters scarcely needed the daily urging from the newspapers, the television, and the omnipresent billboards, to rally and fight. Nor did Maria need to box Pozzo's ears. The Government, struck with panic, did that for her. He was sacked in the most humiliating fashion that could be devised, and in that, at least, the Holy Office took a hand. An article in the Vatican newspaper, written by Di Pino and touched up by Rezzonico, finished Pozzo's career in politics for life.

Then, at the climax of the campaign, Capuano preached his sermon, and the whole country heard him. The next day the tree was destroyed in the presence of a commission representing the Church, the State, and the family welfare organizations throughout the land.

*

One day when it was all over, Joe stretched himself luxuriously on a long chair under the vine-trellis and said to Harry:

'How nice to do nothing again: absolutely nothing. Why don't you settle down here and we'll do nothing together?'

'A week of it would near kill me,' said Harry. 'Besides, I've got plans.'

'Plans?' said Joe, drowsily. 'What plans, Harry?'

'Same plans as I always had ever since I was a little kid. Saving people. I ought to have been a clergyman really, not a biologist. But it seems to me that the time's come to wake people up. They've got to start thinking of right and wrong again, just as they had to a couple of thousand years ago when the Christians took over from the Greeks and the Romans. We've got to start using our brains.'

He went on for a while, but Joe, sleeping lightly in the sunshine, did not hear him. He woke after a few moments.

'Eh?' he said.

'I was asking you if you didn't agree with me,' said Harry.

'Oh yes, yes indeed, I agree,' said Joe. 'But Harry, I'm afraid that if the only way we can be saved is by using our brains, you'll find that we'd all much rather be damned.'

With that he fell asleep and did not wake until Minu called them in to luncheon.